SAMURAI GIRL

BOOK THREE

THE BOOK OF THE PEARL

侍

Carrie Asai

SIMON PULSE
New York London Toronto Sydney Singapore

First Simon Pulse edition September 2003

Text copyright © 2003 by 17th Street Productions, an Alloy company

Interior illustrations copyright © 2003 by Renato Alarcao

SIMON PULSE
An imprint of Simon & Schuster Children's Publishing Division
1230 Avenue of the Americas, New York, NY 10020

 Produced by 17th Street Productions,
an Alloy company
151 West 26th Street
New York, NY 10001

Printed in the United States of America
10 9 8 7 6 5 4 3 2 1

Library of Congress Control Number 2003106779
ISBN: 0-689-86432-9

I wanna check you out
Check you out, hey yo yo
I'm packin' cash like Konishi Kogo
Got my girls in a huddle on the club couch
When I go out I don't need to say much
All the boys they ask, "Where's Heaven at?"
If I knew I'd have to kill you with my gat
Nobody knows where baby has gone
Sing hey, hey . . .

—"Heaven's Gone,"
the newest single from
Tokyo hip-hop band Funkitout

The real nature of ignorance is the
Buddha-nature itself;
The empty illusory body
Is the very body of the Dharma.
　　　　　　—Yungchia Hsuanchueh (665–713)

Tokyo
Daily
News

January 12, 2004

Authorities remain silent about the ongoing investigation of the death of Ohiko Kogo, son of business scion Konishi Kogo (of Kogo Industries fame). Details have been slow to surface in the mysterious death, which took place at the Los Angeles wedding of Kogo's adopted daughter, Heaven, to Takeda "Teddy" Yukemura, son of the prominent Yukemura family. Sources have leaked numerous contradictory details to the press, but the following facts have been verified: an intruder (some say a ninja) invaded the wedding, killing Ohiko Kogo after a violent sword fight witnessed by dozens of guests. Heaven Kogo fled the scene, and it is unclear whether she remains in the United States or has returned to Japan. Several weeks ago Konishi Kogo was flown back to Tokyo in a coma after another reputed ninja attack. Authorities once again refused to comment on rumors that Heaven Kogo may have been involved in the second attack. Konishi Kogo remains in a coma at an undisclosed location. His wife, Mieko, has refused repeated requests for an interview. Heaven Kogo, of course, first caught the nation's attention in 1984 at the age of six months as the sole survivor of Japan Airlines flight 999, which crashed en route from Tokyo to Los Angeles. When no family members surfaced to claim the child, Konishi and Mieko Kogo stepped forward to adopt her. . . .

"Are you sure you know where you're going?" I asked.

"Trust me." Cheryl laughed and tugged at her microscopic denim skirt, which managed to cover even less of her after she pulled it down. I wrapped my sweatshirt around me and scanned the area. We'd hopped off the bus near Second and Alameda—*not* a part of town I'd ever been in. Of course, I'd only been in L.A. for a couple of months, but something told me only Cheryl, my insane roommate, would think she could find a good time in this neighborhood. Still, a ripple of excitement passed through me. It felt good to be out of the house.

"What are those tents?" I asked, pointing to an empty lot crammed full of oddly constructed shacks. Dark figures lurked over a burning trash can, warming themselves against the chilly California night.

"Those are homeless people, Heaven. Don't you have those in Japan?"

"Of—of course," I stuttered, trying to mask my surprise. "Just not—exactly like that." I'd actually never seen a homeless person until I got to the States. I'd grown up in teeming, frenetic Tokyo, but my father's compound was like an oasis in that city. Servants, chauffeured cars, unlimited credit cards, cooks, a gym, a pool—you name it, we had it.

It's a simple story, really, if a little unusual. Baby falls out of a burning plane. Baby named "Heaven" by witty journalist, becomes national celebrity, Japan's "good-luck girl." Baby adopted by Konishi Kogo, head of Kogo Industries and the source of all that wealth I mentioned. Luck holds. Baby grows into Girl. Girl loves father. Girl grows up. Father tells Girl she has to marry Teddy Yukemura, slimy son of business rival. Girl obeys, travels to Los Angeles for hugely elaborate wedding. Wedding crashed by evil ninja. Ninja kills Girl's brother and only ally, Ohiko. Girl flees scene. Luck runs out.

"I think it's this way." Cheryl turned onto a smaller street that was totally devoid of people. I instinctively went into alert mode, casting my senses out like feelers—sort of the same way Spider-Man unfurls his spider goo. (I had developed a huge crush on Tobey Maguire after Cheryl downloaded that movie. Dreamy. Did I mention I'm a total movie-phile?) I didn't sense anything out of the ordinary, but I was still tempted to use some of the stealth techniques I'd

learned just to make sure we got to wherever we were going. I resisted, thinking Cheryl might find it odd if her roomie suddenly began slipping in and out of existence like a ghost. It was just a trick of the eye and mind, really, but it could still be freaky.

Oh—there's one other thing I didn't mention. After Girl went on the lam? Girl became Samurai Girl. Well, Samurai Girl in training. But still.

"Are you sure you know where you're going?" I grabbed Cheryl's jacket and stopped her in her tracks. "There's nothing that even remotely resembles a nightclub here."

"Hehh-vuuuuhn . . . ," Cheryl moaned, rolling her eyes. "Trust me. We agreed that you need this. Remember? All you've been doing for the last week is lying around the house, polluting your mind with bad television and your body with Krispy Kremes."

"I have *not* eaten that many Krispy Kremes," I insisted, laughing. Maybe it was true that I had an unholy affection for the little fried lard puffs. Blame it on the strictly healthy Eastern diet I was raised on. But I wasn't a total addict . . . yet.

"Krispy Kremes aren't even the point. Ever since you and Hiro had that *thing*, which you *still* haven't explained to me, and you got fired from Life Bytes—"

"I did not get *fired*. I quit."

"Whatever. The point is you've been moping around like a sick puppy. You have to get back out there and live a little. Besides, you owe me for this month's rent. That *alone*

6

should be enough to inspire you to hit the job market. And a night at Vibe is going to put you back in action. Trust me." Cheryl's stiletto boots tapped the pavement as she teetered over to the corner and squinted up at the street sign. "Ooh! Peabody. This is it. Let's go."

"I *am* inspired!" I argued as Cheryl skipped off, her cropped blond head (complete with bright pink streaks) bobbing. "But why not just go somewhere on the Strip?" Cheryl ignored me, and I tried to rekindle the feeling of excitement at our big night out. I hated feeling like I wasn't able to take care of myself, having to borrow money (especially from someone like Cheryl, who didn't have a lot of it) when I'd never had to worry about money before. Never even had to consider it. But I was on my own now, and I'd had to quit the first job I'd ever got (at an Internet café) when my almost-husband's family, the Yukemuras, decided they wanted to kidnap me. I was pretty sure by now that the Yukemuras were out to destroy the Kogos and were responsible for my brother's murder. But there were still so many pieces to the puzzle. My brother, who was also my best friend, was dead. My father had been flown back to Japan in a coma, the victim of another ninja attack. And Hiro, my trainer, the man who saved me, was in love with another woman, Karen. And *she* had ended up being kidnapped when she was mistaken for me. I was alone.

How very *Days of Our Lives,* right?

"Wait up!" I called as I caught up with Cheryl, who was speeding toward the faint sound of a thumping bass.

"Okay, Heaven, just be cool," Cheryl whispered theatrically as we turned the corner and saw a bunch of people hanging around outside a nondescript storefront. "Take off that sweatshirt."

"It's freezing," I whined, pulling the sleeves down over my hands. "Besides, I'm not sure about this outfit you made me wear." Cheryl always managed to convince me to wear something I never would normally. Tonight it was a pair of low-slung jeans with a leather belt that sat on my hips and a flowing black top that slid off one shoulder. I'd refused to wear heels, instead choosing a pair of motorcycle boots from Cheryl's vast shoe collection.

I knew I had to be able to run. But more on that later.

"Give it here," Cheryl chirped, ignoring me. She opened her cavernous shoulder bag and held out her hand. I stripped off my sweatshirt and stood there awkwardly, feeling half naked and stupid. Cheryl looked at me critically.

"God, you are one lucky woman. Whatever kind of training you and Hiro do, it's working. Can you say 'Charlie's Angel'?"

"Shut up, dork," I said, blushing. I still wasn't used to getting compliments.

"Okay. Here's the deal," Cheryl said, suddenly all business. "Vibe is underground. That means they don't really have a license to be here, and they only advertise by word of mouth. So we have to be very chill—plus we don't look like hip-hop regulars, so just play it cool. Do you have that ID I gave you?"

I fished in the back pocket of my jeans and pulled out the fake ID Cheryl had made for me. Just having it made me feel instantly cooler, like a "normal" teenager. I suppressed a giggle as I looked at it. There was nothing Cheryl couldn't do. A few weeks before, she'd dragged me into the bathroom and done my makeup, then taken me to a photo booth in a nearby mall for pictures. And now there I was, grinning out from the plastic card, complete with an assumed name—Heaven Johnson. I wasn't sure of my ethnic background, since I was adopted, but it was pretty certain that I was half Caucasian. And with the ID, I'd aged from nineteen to twenty-three overnight—presto! Every inch the California girl.

"All right, let's go," Cheryl said, giving me a last once-over. You would have thought we were about to go into battle. That was one of the things I loved about Cheryl— she took having a good time *seriously.*

The bouncer was sitting on a stool, talking to a few guys in baggy jeans and do-rags. He looked us up and down, then waved us in without another glance. "Have a good time, ladies," he said. I heard one of the guys whistle before the heavy iron door closed behind us. I glanced back, and another guy grinned at me, displaying a row of gold teeth. I looked away quickly and shivered. I hoped Cheryl knew what she was getting us into.

My heart pounded as we descended into the club and the music enveloped us. Whatever was going on at Vibe, I had a feeling I was going to like it.

"This is even better then I thought!" Cheryl yelled, leaning toward me. "You can actually hear yourself think in here. And none of that mind-numbing techno."

I nodded, only half listening, entranced by the sea of bodies on the dance floor. I'd only been to one other club in L.A. (also with Cheryl), and the difference was like night and day. The people at Vibe looked like they were there because they *wanted* to be—not because it was the hippest place to be seen. But they also looked like they *belonged* there somehow, and I wasn't sure we did. A glass bar lit from beneath let out a soothing glow, and red velvet booths lined the walls, each with its own tiny lamp—it had a very retro feel, kind of like what I'd seen in old Hollywood musicals—and the fact that it was underground made if feel almost like a speakeasy. Very Harlem Renaissance. Very mafia. I couldn't quite put my finger on it, but something about the place made me feel like anything could happen—and that the *anything* wouldn't necessarily be good.

"What do you want?" Cheryl asked, squeezing onto a stool at the crowded, glowing bar.

"You pick," I said. I'd been out with Cheryl before, and it was easier to let her deal with the drinks. The one time I'd ordered for myself, I'd ended up with a frothy pink concoction that tasted like cough medicine.

"Stoli Vanilla and Coke?"

"You're the boss."

The drink was delicious. It didn't taste alcoholic at all. I eased back onto my bar stool, bopping a little to the groove, feeling free. The people who stood trying to get the bartenders' attention seemed to embody every hip-hop variation imaginable. Some of the guys looked thuggish, like the ones outside, in their baggy clothes and knit caps, with gold chains in full effect. Others seemed more Rastafarian, wearing dreads and Marley T-shirts. Some of the girls were dressed in standard "club" clothes, like Cheryl and me, and others had blond hair like Eve and impossibly tight jeans. Black, white, Asian, Hispanic—and everything in between—the whole spectrum of color was represented. I felt totally out of my element—and it was a great feeling.

"So what do you think of the club?" Cheryl asked, dancing around a bit. "Do they have anything like this back in Japan?"

"Well, nowhere *I've* ever been to—which isn't saying much." Cheryl nodded understandingly—something else I loved about her. Even though it seemed impossible to her that I'd lived to be nineteen without setting foot in a dance club, she could still be sympathetic. Don't get me wrong—I knew about different "scenes" from a steady (and secret) diet of pop culture magazines and web browsing. I'd just never experienced them.

"But the hip-hop scene is actually pretty huge in Tokyo," I said, taking another delicious sip of my drink. "There's a whole group of kids who spend all day in the tanning salon and then go out to hip-hop clubs with names like Night Avenue and Kingston Club. I always kind of wondered about those places."

"Wait—you mean they go to tanning salons to get darker?"

"Yeah. They want to look like rap stars—or hip-hop stars. And since the most famous ones are black . . ."

"That's really wild. Small world, huh? Culturally, I mean."

"I guess. It's weird, though—the hip-hop thing in Japan is a little more cartoony than this, you know? Like, all the girls get those long acrylic nails, and the boys wear really elaborate coordinated outfits—everyone's just trying to be like what they see in the music videos. It's all about the image. My ex-fiancé was totally like that." I looked around, wondering if Teddy had ever been to this club. It seemed like his type of scene. Teddy had disappeared a few weeks ago, and I had no idea where he was now.

"Vibe seems to be more about the music," I said, pushing thoughts of what might have happened to him away. Worrying about it wasn't going to do any good. "About doing your own thing," I added thoughtfully. I stared out into the throbbing crowd of dancers.

"Hello? Earth to Heaven?"

I shook my head and tried to smile at Cheryl. Sometimes all I wanted was for my brain to shut down. Thinking about all that had happened, and what it meant, never seemed to get me anywhere. "Let's go dance," I said, jumping off my stool.

"Why, Heaven, I thought you'd never ask!"

The dance floor was full, but there was just enough room to move. I felt awkward at first, but when a familiar 50 Cent song came on, I finally let go and got into the groove. It was a remix I hadn't heard, and it made dancing easy— you didn't even have to think about it, your body just *wanted* to move in the right direction. I closed my eyes and let myself go.

"Cut it out, loser!"

My eyes flickered open and I saw Cheryl elbow a thick-looking guy who'd cozied up behind her. He threw his hands up in the air and smiled with a "What?" look on his face.

"Just helping you out, sister," he said.

I stopped dancing, unsure of what to do. I hoped Cheryl wouldn't tick him off with some smart comment.

"Yeah, well, my butt doesn't need your help! Thanks." Cheryl turned her back on the guy, who wiped a hand across his brow in mock nervousness. His friends started laughing.

"They're so desperate!" Cheryl yelled in my ear over the music. "You've got to keep 'em in line."

I laughed. Cheryl was tough. I could learn a lot from her. She joined me in the middle of the dance floor.

"You ladies care to join me?" a short guy with a bald head and a button-up shirt that looked about two sizes too small for him called out from his table, where he sat alone. I wasn't sure how long we'd been dancing, but I didn't really want to stop.

"Not now, baby," Cheryl said, ever the smooth one, as she pulled me toward the bar.

"Why not join *this?*" The man who stepped in front of us gestured to his chest, which was impressively built. "I'm just over there with my peeps." He pointed to one of the red velvet booths that lined the walls of the club. A couple of girls with their boobs hiked up to their ears and several more guys were crammed in there, and they looked unenthused at the prospect of us joining them.

"Looks like you have enough company," Cheryl said, and tried to step around him. Her pursuer blocked the way, his dark eyes shining in the low light.

"Not enough for me." He reached out and grabbed Cheryl's arm.

"Don't touch me!" Cheryl said, the playful tone leaving her voice.

"Hey," I said, stepping forward, "we're not interested." The man looked at me for the first time. "I don't think I was talking to you," he sneered. I opened my mouth to let loose a snappy comeback, but nothing came out. This was Cheryl's territory, not mine. And although I could have taken him out with one kick, the situation certainly didn't call for that. I clapped my mouth shut. As a fighter, I was of some use—as a diplomat? Forget it.

"Look," Cheryl said, flashing me a look that said, *I'll handle this,* "it's a sweet offer, but maybe later, okay?" Her voice had softened, and she slid out of the guy's grasp slowly. "I'm really flattered."

"I may hold you to that," he said with a smile. I breathed with relief. Cheryl had diffused the situation like a pro.

"Great. Later." Cheryl waggled her fingers at him, and he moved toward the bar. I stepped forward.

"Good work," I whispered.

Cheryl tugged at her skirt. "No big deal. You're going to have to get used to stuff like that—Miss Feisty."

"Hey, hey!" I turned around. The short guy with the tight shirt was trying to get our attention again.

"Jeez." I rolled my eyes at Cheryl. "What is *with* these guys?"

"I kind of feel sorry for him—he looks so lost." Cheryl smiled at Shorty and I pulled on the back of her shirt.

"What are you doing?" I said under my breath. "He's the only guy here who looks as nervous as I feel." He gestured wildly with one hand, biting his nails with the other.

"Come on . . . ," Cheryl coaxed, "he looks so lonely. Rule one: If you're going to accept a free drink, accept it from someone harmless."

I sighed. "Okay." I sure knew what feeling out of place was like. And Cheryl was right—this guy was nerd city.

"Come on," he wheedled, "I'll buy you a drink."

"Don't mind if we do," she said. "I'm Cheryl. And this is Heaven."

"I'm Dubious," he said, and held out his hand.

I looked over at Cheryl. Was this guy for real?

"It's a nickname," Dubious explained. "My real name's Gerald." He couldn't stop tapping the table with his fingers. I wondered what he was so worked up about, but I was too shy to ask.

Cheryl wasn't. "What's wrong with you?"

"Just nerves," Dubious replied. "I don't quite know what to say to a couple of pretty girls like you."

"Aw, that's sweet," Cheryl said. "Why not try, 'Hey, let me buy you a couple of drinks'?" I kicked Cheryl's leg under the table.

Dubious frowned. "Oh God, I'm sorry. Drinks. Yes. I'll be right back." He scurried off.

"Cheryl! That was so mean! The poor guy!"

"What? He said he wanted to buy us drinks, so . . . let him!" Cheryl whipped out her compact and reapplied her lipstick.

"I know he did, but he seems so . . . young. He's about as good at talking to women as I am at talking to men."

"So maybe you guys can practice on each other." Cheryl laughed, raising an eyebrow.

"Thanks a *lot,* jerk." Cheryl laughed again.

"Drinks?" Dubious placed two red drinks on the table.

Cheryl began downing hers immediately. I could tell she was already bored with Dubious and wanted to head for greener pastures. I sipped my drink just to be polite. "What is this?" I whispered to Cheryl.

"Vodka cranberry," Cheryl said, then turned to Dubious and raised her glass. "Good choice."

"So what do you do?" I asked Dubious, whose tics seemed to have intensified. He reminded me of Farnsworth, this guy I used to work with at Life Bytes. Maybe I just had a soft spot for nerdy types. They were usually a lot nicer than the hot guys—in my limited experience, anyway. I wondered what Dubious's story was.

"I'm a performer," he said.

"Were you on *American Idol*?" Cheryl asked. I kicked her again. Why was she giving him such a hard time?

Dubious's face lit up. "No, but I tried out for that show!"

"You *did?*" I asked, amazed to have run into someone who would actually subject themselves to that kind of humiliation. Maybe Dubious was just a glutton for punishment. After all, millions of Japanese were. On our reality shows, a lot worse things happened. Like, they'd film this guy walking up to people and screaming in their faces, scaring the crap out of them. Literally. And that was the least of it.

"Yep. Paula liked me, but Simon said I was a ridiculous excuse for a human being, let alone a pop star."

"Ouch," I said.

"What did you sing?" Cheryl asked.

"'Lady Marmalade,'" Dubious said, then launched into a falsetto rendition, *"Mocha-choca-latta-ya-ya."* I chewed my lip in a desperate attempt not to laugh, and I saw that Cheryl was digging her nails into her arm for the same reason.

"Wow," Cheryl said, trying to keep a straight face, "I can't believe you didn't make it."

"I know." Dubious sighed. "But someday I will." He gulped at his drink, slumping in his chair a little bit.

"You will," I said, and patted his shoulder.

"You really think so?" he asked, his face brightening.

"Definitely," Cheryl chimed in. "Okay, Dubious, we gotta go."

"So soon?"

"Sorry, things to do." Cheryl stood up.

"Bye!" I yelled over my shoulder as Cheryl dragged me away from the table. When I looked back a moment later, Dubious had already found another unsuspecting victim, so I didn't feel that bad.

"What's up with *that* guy?" Cheryl asked, and we both burst out laughing.

"Do you think he comes here a lot?" I asked.

"Probably. Every club has its weirdoes, even the cool ones. There are some very lonely people in L.A."

Don't I know it, I thought as Cheryl and I wove through the smoky club toward the bathrooms. Two girls cut in front of me after Cheryl went in, but I was too much of a wuss to say anything. Loneliness washed over me. I thought about

Hiro and how he'd hate it if he knew I was at a place like this. Sometimes it seemed like Cheryl was the only person I could be real with—and that was pretty pathetic, considering there were a million things about myself I couldn't tell her. What kind of friendship was that?

Cheryl picked up another drink for herself on our way back to the dance floor. The bartender who served her had a shaved head and huge hoop earrings and looked like she would be at home on a Milan runway. She was cool, calm, and collected. The opposite of how I felt, which was about twelve years old. Cheryl downed her drink as quickly as the one Dubious had given her.

"Are you sure you should be drinking all that?" I couldn't help asking.

"Don't be so . . . ," Cheryl said, tracing a little air square with her fingers. "Come on, let's dance."

So we did. I had no idea how long we were out there; I only knew that it felt incredible to let loose and dance. My mind went totally blank as I let my body follow the beat all on its own. The only time over the last few months I'd even come close to such mental peace was when I tried out some of Hiro's meditation techniques. Dancing at Vibe blew meditation away.

When I opened my eyes, Cheryl was gone. I had no idea how long I'd been dancing, but it felt like a huge weight had been lifted from my shoulders. This was the America I'd wanted to be a part of so long ago, and I felt miles away from all my troubles. Somehow I didn't feel as lonely any-more. I scanned the dance floor and caught sight of a pink-streaked head. A slow song had come on, and Cheryl was dancing with someone. Actually, dancing wasn't the right word—they were so close, it was hard to tell where Cheryl ended and the guy began. He turned, and I saw that he was gorgeous. Tall and trim, with skin the color of a mocha latte.

When the song ended, Cheryl whispered something in her new friend's ear, then walked over to me.

"Marcus and I are going to go talk," Cheryl said, and winked.

"That's Marcus, I presume?" I giggled.

"Isn't he adorable? I love a man with style."

"That suit he's wearing looks like Versace," I said. I used to follow high fashion back in Japan. Actually, I used to *wear* high fashion back in Japan. My father wasn't always the most lovable man in the world, but he wasn't stingy. Of course, I was rarely allowed to get the kind of cutting-edge outfits I wanted, but I made do. At least my father didn't usually object to Juicy Couture hoodies and Seven jeans.

"Here." Cheryl squeezed a twenty-dollar bill into my hand. "Get a drink. I'll be back in a little while."

"Be careful," I said, smiling. "And thanks!" I yelled as she walked away.

"Okay. But not *too* careful," Cheryl said, looking over her shoulder with a grin.

I figured I'd burned off my other two drinks with all that

dancing, so I ordered a vodka and cranberry juice, which tasted delicious. I was so thirsty that I ordered another one, drank it down, then surveyed the scene. It was three in the morning, according to the bar clock, but I wasn't tired at all. I felt more relaxed then I'd been since—well, since ever. I slid off my stool and got back on the dance floor, totally giving myself up to the music and the soft red light that made all the dancers look like ghosts. It felt so good to use my body this way, so different from the rigidity and force required by my martial arts training. I let the music flow through me, imagining I could feel it tingling all the way down to my toes. I felt *real* at Vibe. Not exactly safe, but more like the old Heaven, the one who would dance around in her room by herself just for fun, the one who dreamed of coming to college in the States, the one who dreamed of new adventures. I wanted that Heaven back, and on the dance floor it actually seemed possible to find her. I never wanted the music to end.

Suddenly I felt a pair of arms slide around my waist.

"Hey!" I yelled, trying to see behind me. Some guy had latched himself around me like a python.

"You're too hot," he whispered in my ear, still bumping and grinding against me.

I gulped and scanned the dance floor. I was on my own. So the question was: What would Cheryl do in this situation?

I eased out of his grip and turned to face my pursuer. He

was one of the Rastafarians, with dreads and a knit cap. He put a hand on my hip and tried to draw me closer.

"H-Hey, now," I stammered, trying to keep it light, "you can look but don't touch."

He let go of my waist and held both hands in the air, smiling. It was working!

"But you look so fine," he said, leaning toward me. I was flattered in spite of myself. Why not dance with him? I had nothing better to do, and if Cheryl could take care of herself—maybe I could, too.

Eventually my new partner excused himself to get a drink, and I stayed on the dance floor, fending off more partners. After a while I got downright slick about it. A guy would come up and start rubbing himself all over me, and I'd just smile, hold out an arm, and push him gently away— still dancing with him but at a safe distance. They'd stay for a song or so and then move on to greener pastures. It was kind of fun learning how to flirt this way.

"Hey, Dancing Queen!" Cheryl tapped my shoulder. I looked around and noticed the club had cleared out considerably.

"What time is it?" I asked, feeling a little out of it. How long had she been gone?

"Just after four. Closing time."

"I can't believe it. I feel great." I stretched out my arms and blinked. I was sweaty and tired, but in the best possible way.

"Me too. Listen—before we go, there's someone I want you to meet."

I trailed Cheryl back to the bar, where Marcus was talking to a bartender. His suit was cut to perfection, accentuating his broad shoulders and trim waist. Very Vin Diesel. I grabbed a napkin and wiped my sweaty forehead. Not the sexiest maneuver, but I was feeling too good to care.

"Heaven, meet Marcus. And this is his friend A. J.," Cheryl said, gesturing to the bartender.

"Hi." Marcus smiled. I reached out to shake his hand and noticed he was wearing a large gold ring studded with rubies.

"Great to meet you, Heaven," he said, looking down at me. He had to be six-two at least, and Cheryl looked almost like a little kid next to him. "We hear you're looking for a job."

"Ummm . . . yeah," I said, a little embarrassed. I wondered why Cheryl had felt the need to tell them I was unemployed.

"We're really hurting for some help," A.J. said, leaning over the bar. "Do you think you'd want to work here?"

"At Vibe?" I said stupidly.

"Yep. We need someone to pass out shots on the dance floor. No experience necessary. All you have to do is give out the shots and collect five bucks apiece. I'll even teach you how to make them."

"Uh—"

"Doesn't that sound awesome?" Cheryl interrupted before I could get a word out. Marcus draped his Versace-clad arm around her and smiled his strange smile at me again. "And A. J. said then you'll get in for free whenever you want. Obviously." Cheryl seemed as excited as if *she* was the one who was going to work here.

"It *does* sound great . . . ," I mumbled, "but . . ."

"Listen," A. J. said, running his hand through his hair in a gesture that reminded me of Hiro, "Cheryl told us you have a little documentation problem, but it doesn't matter. We pay strictly under the table. You'll get four bucks an hour plus all your tips. And I think you can look forward to *a lot* of tips." A. J. gave me an approving look. "On a busy night you'll make three hundred bucks—easy."

"Excellent," I said, trying to keep from smiling like an idiot. I hadn't been sure about how to bring up the whole "illegal alien" thing, but Cheryl seemed to have worked all that out, too. "When do I start?"

"How about tomorrow at ten?"

"Perfect." I wanted to dance. I'd gotten lucky again! Someone had given me a job even though I had no experience and no papers. And I'd get to come to Vibe almost every day! I couldn't imagine a job more fun than *that*.

"Okay. See you tomorrow, then." A. J. moved away to finish closing down the bar, and Marcus gave Cheryl a slow kiss. I looked away, concentrating on the bottles lined up neatly behind the bar. I couldn't help thinking that I'd never been kissed like that. An image of Hiro flashed across my brain. *Don't be greedy, Heaven,* I told myself, *you've got a job, and that's enough for now.*

"It was nice to meet you, Heaven," Marcus said. His voice was as slow and smooth as his smile. Cheryl grabbed my arm, and with one last longing look at Marcus and his hot bod, we were off.

"Ohmigod, ohmigod, ohmigod!" Cheryl squealed, doing a funky little two-step in the middle of the street. "Isn't Marcus the hottest thing you've ever seen?"

"Totally." I laughed, linking arms with Cheryl. "And you are the *best* roommate in the universe. I can't believe you got me a job at Vibe!"

"Thass right," Cheryl said, slurring her words a little bit. I wondered how much she'd had to drink. I was feeling a little giddy myself, but Cheryl was really unsteady on her feet. "We both got something we needed." She whirled out of my grasp and spun around in the abandoned street. "Marcus is so *fine!*" she yelled, her words echoing through the abandoned neighborhood.

I laughed, but I couldn't help thinking of Hiro. Why was love so easy for everyone else?

"What's wrong?" Cheryl asked, latching onto me again as we continued down the street.

"I'm sorry. I was just thinking about Hiro. And Karen." Karen was a teacher at the same dojo where Hiro trained. More importantly, she was now Hiro's girlfriend—and she was beautiful. Cheryl knew all that. What she didn't know was that a few weeks ago, Karen had been accidentally kidnapped by the people who were after me. I'd barely seen Hiro at all since we rescued her. Long story.

"Forget him!" Cheryl yelled. "What does she have that you don't? A thousand guys at Vibe were checking you out tonight. You need to expand your horizons. Play the field. Besides, Karen sounds like a boring little lame ass. You need a guy who knows how to have fun. Like Marcus."

I laughed. It was impossible to be jealous of Cheryl. She had a big heart, and without her I'd be both homeless and jobless. "I'm so happy for you," I said. "He really seems great."

"He knows absolutely everybody," Cheryl raved. "He has his own events company. He planned a party for P. Diddy."

"Seriously?" I asked, impressed.

"Yes. If things work out with us, we're going to be hitting some of the hottest parties in L.A. Won't that be awesome?"

"Totally." I readjusted my hold on Cheryl, who was leaning on me pretty heavily now. When my brother, Ohiko, and I used to talk about coming to the States together, we'd just assumed we'd meet lots of celebrities, but I hadn't seen even one since coming to L.A. I guess that wasn't too surprising, given that I'd spent most of my time at Hiro's apartment, or in the dojo, or getting attacked by ninjas. I indulged in a quick fantasy of myself at a swank celebrity party, the kind I was always reading about in US magazine, chatting up Maggie and Jake Gyllenhall or having a drink on the balcony with Leonardo DiCaprio. Maybe this was the beginning of a totally new life for me.

A loud noise ripped through the early morning silence, jolting me back down to earth. I broke out in goose bumps. Cheryl and I stopped in our tracks.

"Wha . . . ?" Cheryl whispered, confused. The noise had sounded like something being overturned—a trash can, maybe, or a Dumpster? I came back to reality with a thud. I let go of Cheryl and concentrated on the sounds of the street, listening for any changes in the pattern of noises— the faraway rumbling of the highway, the creak of a loose street sign moving in the night wind. Samurai training was teaching me to use my senses to the fullest—so much so that sometimes it seemed like I was using a new, sixth sense. The streets were empty, but I sensed someone lurking in the shadows. I just knew it wasn't safe here.

"How far are we from the bus stop?" I whispered. L.A. was a real pain in the ass without a car. Not that either of us was in driving condition—and not that I had a driver's license. I vowed to take a driver's ed class as soon as my life calmed down. Whenever that might be.

"A few blocks, I think," Cheryl said, squinting and looking around. "There's one on Alameda."

"Are we close to a subway stop?" I felt nervous about waiting at a bus stop, where we'd be exposed. I'd never been on the subway in L.A. Unfortunately, it didn't seem to go anywhere I needed to go.

"Nobody takes the subway except teenagers from the Valley," Cheryl scoffed. "Besides, it doesn't run all night."

"Okay, let's just get to the bus stop." I grabbed Cheryl's arm and steered her forward.

"Hey! What's the rush?" One of Cheryl's stilettos got caught between the sidewalk cracks and she yelped. "I've got to get these things off," she said, and made as though she was going to sit down on the pavement.

"Cheryl—no. Come on. We're almost there." I tried to grab her under the shoulders and she cackled loudly. "Shhh," I murmured, looking around. Cheryl swallowed her laugh with mock seriousness, holding up one finger in front of her pursed lips.

Just then another noise echoed through the streets. I stiffened. It sounded like footsteps.

"Oh, please, Heaven. My feet are killing me. I just want to—"

"Come on, let's go," I hissed, pulling her to her feet. Cheryl didn't argue. We scurried down the street and made a quick left. That's when I saw them.

Two men. Shadowy in the just-before-dawn darkness.

Glints of silver in their hands. I felt the familiar terror slide through me, the realization that an attack was about to begin. I let the feeling rest inside me without fighting it, tried to use it to assess the situation.

"Give it up," said the shorter one, his knife glittering. "Throw all your cash on the ground. And your jewelry."

I breathed a sigh of relief—which might seem weird, seeing as how I was being mugged. These weren't yakuza hit men, and they certainly weren't ninja. Who would have thought it could feel so good to be just another victim of random violence?

"We don't have any," I said, concentrating on making my voice sound clear and unafraid. "All I've got is a bus pass."

"Nope, nope," Cheryl echoed, waving her head tipsily back and forth.

"Don't play with us, man. This ain't no joke. Hand it over!" The taller of the two muggers stepped forward menacingly. His movements were jerky, and he looked nervously behind him as he barked at us. "Now!"

I was pretty sure they were on some kind of drugs, and I took that into account as I planned my defense. On the plus side, it meant an attack would be sloppier. On the minus—they'd be less conflicted about hurting us. I felt strong and hoped it wasn't just a false sense of security brought on by all of my vodka cranberries.

"Oh, man," groaned the little one. "Let's just take 'em

down and get the money. We gotta get out of here." He pulled his baseball cap lower over his eyes and hopped from left foot to right.

"Look—I have nothing to give you," I said. "Why don't you just leave us alone?"

"I don't think you heard me, bitch," growled the tall one, who was obviously the leader of their little gang of two. I stared at him evenly. No one had ever spoken to me like that. I felt anger searing through my veins.

"No, I don't think you heard *me*," I said, surprised at the steely sound of my own voice. "My friend and I have no money. No cash, no jewelry, no nothing. So you're going to have to find someone else to rob."

"Oh, man, I can't believe this." The short one clawed at his friend's coat. "Let's just go, man, come on." I realized he couldn't be much more than sixteen, and all of a sudden I felt a little sorry for them. They couldn't even mug someone right.

"We're not going anywhere," the tall one said, shrugging his friend off like a fly. "You're going to be one sorry little piece of—"

He lunged toward me, his knife held in front of him. Instinctively I pushed Cheryl to the ground and, in the same motion, delivered a roundhouse kick that knocked the knife out of his hand. For a split second he had no idea what hit him. He ducked down to recover his knife and I aimed another kick, this one short and level, at his chin, being

careful to gauge my force so that I wouldn't break his jaw.
He flew backward and landed with a thud in the street just
as his little buddy joined the fight. I bent my knees and
braced for what was coming.

"Heaven!" Cheryl screamed, warning me.

"Stay down, Cheryl!" I blurted without looking at her.
The little guy looked scared.

"Why don't you just get out of here?" I asked, hoping to
avoid any more fighting. "We won't call the cops."

"Screw you!" he yelled, and came toward me, flailing
around with his knife. He took a wild, easily avoidable stab
at me, and I stepped aside, grabbing his arm and twisting
it, locking him in a grip from which he couldn't escape. I
delivered three short punches to his face, and the knife fell
from his hands. When I released him, he stumbled backward, cradling his bleeding forehead in disbelief.

"Go!" I screamed. And he did, along with his partner. A
surge of power washed over me as I watched their hasty
retreat. Maybe I was beginning to like this fighting thing a little
too much. I grabbed both of the knives from the ground and
clicked them shut, then shoved them in my sweatshirt pocket.

"Come on, Cheryl," I said, helping her up from the
ground. "We've got to get out of here." Cheryl stood obedi-
ently, staring at me like I was an alien.

"What?" I asked, but I knew what.

"That was incredible! That was amazing! You just kicked
two guys' asses!"

"Luck," I said, dragging her down the street. "Cheryl, we really have to get to the bus stop. Those kids might come back with reinforcements. Besides, it's starting to get light out."

"I'm coming, I'm coming," Cheryl gasped, and we power walked to the bus stop. "I knew you and Hiro did martial arts training, but that was like—like *Street Fighter* or something! You're the original Chun-Lee!"

"Except not Chinese," I said wryly.

"You know what I mean." Cheryl's breath was ragged from our speed walk, but she couldn't let the topic rest.

"The bus!" I yelled with relief as I spotted it lumbering toward us. "I can't believe it's actually coming!" Sometimes I felt like I spent more time in L.A. *waiting* for the bus than actually *riding* it—and that was during daylight hours. If we let this one go, who knew when another would come along? I sprinted toward the stop, half dragging Cheryl behind me.

"Come on, Cheryl!"

Cheryl staggered the last few feet and I hauled her up the steps. Panting, we stumbled toward a couple of seats in the back. A few working people on their way to early shifts looked at us sleepily but without interest. I collapsed into the seat and stared out the window as the ugly streets of downtown L.A. came into soft focus. I knew the adrenaline would wear off within a few minutes, and I'd be left exhausted and spent. Fighting was the ultimate workout, I'd had the misfortune to learn over the past few months. But Cheryl wasn't finished with me yet.

"Where did you learn to do that?" Cheryl asked with awe.

"I'm half Japanese. It's in my blood."

"How can you joke around about this? We could have gotten seriously messed up back there. And you took those two guys out like it was nothing. I mean, I knew you could take care of yourself—but that was something else entirely."

"Seriously, Cheryl," I said, trying to be honest but knowing that I could never tell her the truth, "it's not as cool as it seems. Those guys didn't know what they were doing. I think they were on drugs or something. They were just two stupid kids with knives, and I know a few self-defense moves. Basic stuff."

"Well, it didn't seem basic to me. And now that I think about it, the last time wasn't basic, either."

"The last time was nothing," I said. "I just got lucky twice." A few months ago, before Cheryl and I were roommates, we'd gone dancing at another club and run into some real jerks. They got a little overzealous, and I'd clocked one of them before Cheryl and I dodged out of the place. Looking back, I could see I'd overreacted. If I'd had more of Cheryl's people skills, we probably could have talked our way free of them. I sighed. "It all just seems cooler to you because you're a little wasted."

"I don't think so," Cheryl said, her eyes glowing. "I know a good ass kicking when I see it." Cheryl launched into her version of events, and I let her ramble on and on as the bus rumbled toward Hollywood and home. By the time we got back to the house we shared on Dawson Street, it was almost six in the morning, and even Cheryl was spent. I collapsed into my bed, thinking groggily how lucky it was that Hiro and I hadn't scheduled an early morning aikido workout for today.

I had three hours to sleep. *Well,* I thought as I slipped off, *Cheryl promised me a big night out, and that's exactly what I got.* I also thought, *Please, let me dream of Hiro,* before I could stop myself.

But I was too tired to dream.

So Heaven has moved on. Interesting. I thought for certain she'd be home by now, scared to death of the prospect of being on her own, without her father's protection, without his support. This has changed everything, this continued absence of hers. I'll have to think carefully about how to woo her back, woo her out. Perhaps this friend of Heaven's has information that can be bought. Everyone has a price.

Mine was high.

Konishi grows paler every day. I visit him in the private clinic, sit by his side, watching the blips of the machines, holding his cold hand in mine. His time is running out, too. I wonder if he knows it. I wonder if he can think at all inside the misty prison of his coma. Sometimes I whisper my thoughts in his ear, and at those moments it seems I can almost see a trembling in his eyelids, the jerk of a muscle in his jaw.

Yes, I think he hears me. I think he hears the hiss of the match catching fire, the almost silent crackle of the tobacco in my cigarette as I light it. The trickle of liquid as a drink is poured. The rasp of a nail file. I believe that he hears all of this.

It has been many months since the wedding, since the day that my son, my blood *child, Ohiko, was murdered. Sometimes I imagine that I see him still, turning a corner, staring from the window of a train, a shop, a house. It's all Heaven's fault. She brought nothing but bad luck into the home Konishi and Ohiko and I shared. Before she arrived, I was happy. She brought too many secrets with her.*

She must be kept safe at all costs. I have to see her again, to find her and tell her all the same things that I whisper into Konishi's ear here at the clinic. I dream of that moment as I caress my husband's hand. But Konishi's ki is ebbing away. Time is running out.

I must find her again. Heaven may have learned how to fly away, but she has nowhere safe to land.

Mieko

3

As soon as I stepped on the bus, things started to go wrong. I had forgotten my bus pass, probably in the pants I'd hurled onto the floor when Cheryl and I got home at dawn.

"Exact change, honey," the bored-looking bus driver said.

"I know. Yes. Maybe these people could go first?" I pleaded, blushing as I pawed through my knapsack, looking for loose change. The bus driver ignored me, even when I stepped aside to let the grumbling people behind me through.

"Get it together, Karate Girl. This ain't no free ride," said an older woman as she pushed past me, her arms cluttered with bags, and almost knocked me over.

I managed to find the right amount of change before starting a riot, but as soon as I squeezed into a seat, a blanket of

fatigue dropped over me, and I could barely keep my eyes open as the bus picked its way through the early morning traffic. I tried to think about some of the moves Hiro and I had been practicing lately, but my mind wandered, and the high I'd been on when I woke up started to fade. I had a job, yes, but—that was about all I had. Things hadn't really changed that much. I tried to talk myself back into my earlier exhilaration, but it was gone. *At least you're back at the dojo,* I told myself. When the Yukemuras were after me, the dojo hadn't been a safe place for Hiro and me to train anymore. But Hiro and I figured it was okay for the time being, seeing as how Teddy was out of the picture—and the bottom line was, if the Yukemuras wanted to find me, they were going to find me no matter where I went. They'd already proved that. At least the dojo was comforting.

"Good morning, Heaven."

I clicked back to reality with a jerk. Somehow I'd floated into the dojo's practice room without even registering that I wasn't still on the bus. Uh-oh. I was really sleepwalking.

"Hey, Hiro," I said, throwing my bag down and watching Hiro stretch. Hiro's body was perfect. There was no other word for it. I couldn't have dreamed up a more ideal-looking guy. He was about six feet tall, which was a great height for me, at five-nine—I could look up to him, but he didn't tower over me—and his body was cut from years of martial arts training—he was muscled and wiry but not bulky in that gross, Mr. Universe kind of way.

I sighed to myself. Fantasizing about Hiro would only bring disappointment. I had to move on.

"How's Karen doing?" I forced myself to ask. It wasn't that I didn't care at all—I did—and I felt responsible for what she'd gone through. It was just that talking about her was painful. It made Hiro and Karen's relationship more *real*—and every time I mentioned her name, I felt like Hiro could see right through me.

"Much better," Hiro said, his voice softer. A look of affection flitted across his face. "She's finally getting back to her normal schedule."

"Great," I choked, fumbling in my backpack for nothing just so that I wouldn't have to look at him.

"Should we get going?" Hiro asked. I turned around, watching him push his longish dark hair out of his eyes. "I have a two o'clock shift."

"Sure," I answered, and moved into the center of the room for some stretching. Hiro worked as a bike messenger, a job he enjoyed because it gave him the opportunity to work out *and* meditate. What a guy.

"You feeling okay?" Hiro asked. "You look a little tired."

"Yeah, I'm fine," I said curtly. "Let's just get going." I was finding it hard not to be rude to him—I didn't want to, but the words just came out salty. I took a deep breath. *Control it, Heaven,* I told myself. *Just let it go.* It wasn't Hiro's fault he wasn't obsessed with me like I was with him. But it was hard to fight the pain of rejection. Being with Hiro was simultaneously the most rewarding part of my life and the most excruciating. The truth was, even though I knew he was with Karen, I found it impossible to give up hope. Couldn't he see that we were meant for each other? At least, I was meant for him. The only problem seemed to be that I handled my crush like a third grader. *What are you going to do next, Heaven,* I asked myself, *start throwing spitballs at him to get him to like you?*

"Right," said Hiro, his smile fading, and his voice assuming the businesslike tone it did whenever we trained. "I thought we'd practice some jujitsu moves today. You had so much success with shinobi-iri—but both your mind and your body have been severely strained lately. So instead of working on offensive power moves or resistance against force, we're going to switch gears and work on redirection of force. And that's really what jujitsu is all about."

Shinobi-iri—those ninja invisibility skills I talked about earlier. Turned out I had a knack for it—Hiro said some people never mastered that kind of ninja stealth even with a whole lifetime of training. I couldn't help feeling proud.

"You know," Hiro continued, "jujitsu is really out of favor in Japan right now. It's associated with thugs."

"Hmmm . . . ," I replied dreamily, "sounds about right."

"What do you mean?" Hiro asked, looking confused.

"Well, I seem to run into a lot of thugs, don't I? Maybe I'm becoming thuggish, too." *Stop feeling sorry for yourself, Heaven!* I scolded myself. But a wash of loneliness was making me say things I didn't really mean.

"Ah." Hiro tilted his head and studied me. "Are you sure you're feeling all right? You seem a little out of it."

"Really, Hiro, I'm fine," I said, trying to make my voice sound gentle and apologetic. "Can we just get started?"

Hiro nodded, and we were off. The first hour everything went fairly smoothly. I was a little slow and dopey, and making the readjustment to the new style of fighting was challenging. Until recently Hiro and I had spent all our time preparing for my dustup with the Yukemura hit men. That demanded stealth and an aggressive, power-generating style of attack. The sparring Hiro and I were doing now was all about balance and equilibrium.

Then things started to go wrong. It was as though my body wasn't even connected to my mind anymore. I'd think about spinning left to avoid Hiro's strike, and my feet would get twisted around each other, making me stumble. I'd throw my weight in one direction, only to realize I'd overcalculated. Hiro worked his way past my defenses again and again. Finally, before I could even register what was happening, he flipped me over his shoulder onto the mat.

"Oomph," I grunted, kind of happy just to be lying down. I breathed in the rubbery smell of the mat as though I was lying in a bed of flowers.

"Okay, I think you're *kind of* getting it," Hiro said skeptically.

"Overstatement," I joked from the floor. Hiro ignored me.

"As long as you're down there—I wanted to work on

gatame waza today anyway—ground techniques. We haven't really done anything with that yet."

"Like, ground fighting?" I said, having trouble arranging my confused thoughts. Why would I want to fight on the ground? I propped myself up on one elbow and looked at Hiro. He was just as dreamy from below.

"Yes. It can be especially helpful if you're knocked down, obviously, or held down and find yourself in a position where a simple kick won't free you. Or, of course, if you and your opponent are in a closed space together, say, a car trunk, or if you get thrown into a body of water or something."

"Okay, mafioso." I giggled, forgetting my exhaustion for a minute. "Is there something you're not telling me? You in trouble with Tony Soprano?"

"A samurai must be prepared for every eventuality. You know that," Hiro said seriously, ignoring my joke. Sometimes (often, actually) his sense of humor went into total remission. I doubted he knew who Tony Soprano was—Hiro didn't go in much for TV. I wondered how he and Karen compromised about that—I knew from experience that she enjoyed watching a good, cheesy romantic comedy now and again. I sighed. What I wouldn't give to be lying at home on the couch falling asleep to a video right now—curled up in *someone's* arms.

"I know. Okay." I retied my hair in the futile hope that it would make me feel more awake.

"Good," Hiro said, watching me patiently. "Let's start from a ground position, then."

I gestured vaguely at myself. "I'm here already, you know."

"Okay," Hiro said, crouching down next to me, "roll over on your side. I'm going to put you in a neck hold . . ." Hiro scooted behind me and put his arms around my neck. He smelled like shaving cream and sweat. A good smell. I tried to inhale without being obvious and let my eyes close.

". . . and a leg lock." Hiro entwined his legs with mine. I could feel my face growing hot, and I was glad Hiro was behind me so he couldn't see the blush I knew was there. Why couldn't I stop acting like a love-starved teenager? *Because you* are *a love-starved teenager,* I thought. Not for long, though. My twentieth birthday was just around the corner—at least, the day my family had chosen to celebrate my birthday. For all I knew, I was twenty years old already. And what did I have to show for it? It was too depressing to even think about.

"Now use your elbow first to break the neck hold—that's the most important," Hiro said, and described the series of movements he wanted me to do. I went through them slowly, but when we tried for real, without Hiro giving up any force, I failed miserably. My arms felt like they were made out of jelly.

"Try again," Hiro said, sounding irritated as he repositioned himself.

I tried again and failed. On top of my total exhaustion, having Hiro wrapped around me was just too distracting for words.

"Sorry," I muttered as Hiro untangled himself and faced me. "I'm on the weak side today."

"I don't get it, Heaven. This isn't that hard. Why aren't you trying?" Hiro's mouth drew down around the edges, marring his gorgeous face.

"I *am* trying, Hiro. It's just—why do you think I can do every single thing you teach me right off the bat?" I sat up, hating the whining sound in my voice.

"Because you have the talent to do it. And right now you're just wasting my time." Hiro walked over to his bag and took out his water bottle.

"Well, *excuse* me for being tired," I lashed out. "I have things on my mind."

"Like what?" Hiro said. Normally I would have confided in him, but right then I couldn't. After all, he (and his stupid relationship with stupid Karen) was a big part of the problem.

"Like none of your business," I said petulantly, burying my head in my arms. I just wanted to sleep—to take back the whole stinking morning and start over tomorrow.

"Stop being such a baby, Heaven," Hiro said curtly. "You promised me you would be honest with me, and now you're just acting like a child."

I shrugged, my face still buried in my arms. I just

didn't have the energy to get into a fight with Hiro. I felt beaten, both mentally and physically. My muscles ached, I was nauseated from the drinks I'd had the night before (I stupidly hadn't eaten any breakfast), and my mind was mush. I felt like there was a black cloud hanging over me and me only.

"You seem so depressed, Heaven," Hiro said, his voice softer. He walked over to me, knelt down, and put his hand on my shoulder. "You're not yourself today. What can I do?"

"What do you care?" I blurted, whipping my head up to face him. How dare he pretend to give a crap! It was too little too late. "I was mugged last night. I have no family. Someone's trying to kill me. And I'm broke. So that's *my* life." *And you're too busy with being shmoopy-faced with shmoopy Miss Perfect Karen to even notice,* I added to myself.

"You were mugged?" Hiro asked, his face tightening. "Where?"

I told him about the night before, leaving out the late hour and the neighborhood, figuring I didn't need a lecture from Hiro about being more responsible for my own safety.

"You're sure they weren't yakuza?" Hiro pressed, still looking concerned.

"Hiro." I shook my head. "Don't you think at this point I can tell the difference between two-bit street criminals and professional hit men? These guys were scared—they couldn't fight at all. And I'm sure they were on something."

Hiro sighed. "Well, that sounds like just bad luck, then. I'm sorry you had to go through that. But I think I know something that will help you."

My heart skipped a beat—was Hiro going to suggest something fun, like doing our training session at the beach, like we once had, or taking a trip out of L.A.?

"I think it's time for your next mission," Hiro said, and sat cross-legged in front of me. My heart sank. He was in sensei mode now. Hiro had given me two missions so far, and completing each had been harder than I'd ever imagined possible. The thing about the missions was, you almost couldn't do anything proactive to complete them. You had to just contemplate, and think, and try different things, and then all at once you seemed to "get it." They made life very frustrating sometimes, but Hiro was convinced they were an important aspect of my training. And I had to admit—they were helpful in getting me out of some tight situations. But I really needed a break.

I also couldn't help thinking that if it was *Karen* who'd been mugged, Hiro wouldn't be quite so nonchalant about it.

"Well," continued Hiro, "you know that each mission has do to with some aspect of the bushido—"

"The way of the samurai," I intoned in a singsong voice. Duh. Like I didn't know that. Irritation bubbled inside me. I wanted to shake him out of his professor mode.

"—so because you've been so worried and upset lately—" Hiro said, ignoring my sarcasm, "and with good reason, don't get me wrong—and distracted, your mission is simply to clear your mind."

"Clear my mind?" I asked hollowly. "You mean, like, think about snow falling or waves crashing? Listen to some new age music?"

"Not exactly, although there are tools that you can use to help you. You already know that bushido has its roots in Zen Buddhism—and in Zen, meditation is key. You've already started in on that stuff, I know. There are certain Zen koan, or riddles, that Zen monks use to help them clear their minds of all unnecessary thoughts. I'm sure you've heard the one, 'What's the sound of one hand clapping?'"

"Yeah, I've heard that one," I said, trying to focus. I was getting groggier and groggier and more and more resistant to this little lesson. It was like someone telling you what medicine to take to recover from a cold when really all you wanted was a hug and a little attention.

"Here's another one," Hiro said, "that you can use this week: Someone asked, 'What do you think about? The moment discrimination arises, one becomes confused and loses one's mind?' The Master said, 'Kill, kill!'" Hiro stopped and looked at me as though waiting for me to say something.

A dense, mind-crushing fog settled over my brain. I

could almost feel myself shedding IQ points. Hiro's words made no sense to me.

"I don't get it," I said, my eyes welling up.

"You're not supposed to. That's the whole point. Just remember that the goal is to make your mind as smooth and blank as a pearl."

"Oh," I said dumbly. Somehow I sensed the blankness Hiro was talking about wasn't the blankness I was feeling just then. My head was swimming. I just wanted to go home.

"All right," Hiro said, standing up and collecting his things. "I think that's enough for today. Get some rest, and I'll see you tomorrow at seven for aikido in the park."

"Um . . . about th-that . . . ," I stuttered, the fog clearing for a second. "I'm only going to be able to train in the afternoons now."

"Why?" Hiro asked, not looking pleased. "That's not really convenient for me."

"Well, sorry," I said snottily, flipping my hair and throwing my towel into my knapsack, "but I have a new job, and I work nights. So there's nothing I can do about it."

Hiro's face brightened. "Heaven, that's great! I had no idea! Where are you working?"

Without turning around, I answered, "At this club called Vibe. I'm a shot girl. It's great—people buy shots from me and I collect the money and get to keep all the tips. I could make three hundred dollars a night—and it's totally under the table. I—" I stopped short. Hiro's face was suddenly angry. What had I done? I hadn't planned on telling him where I worked— it was the exhaustion that made me slip up.

"Are you crazy?" Hiro snapped, taking a few steps toward me. "That is *not* the kind of job you should be taking. You're not even twenty-one!"

"So? They don't care. Besides, I have an ID." My sleepiness had vanished and now I was just plain mad. As far as Hiro was concerned, nothing I tried to do was right. I was sick of not living up to his expectations, sick of him treating me like a machine instead of a girl.

"That job is demeaning and . . . and unsafe . . . and totally against everything that a samurai should be striving for!" Hiro ran his hands through his hair. "And I suppose you were mugged coming back from work last night, huh? At what time? Three, four in the morning? How could you lie to me?"

I ignored Hiro's questions and let my anger and bitterness do the talking. "What the hell am I supposed to do, Hiro? How am I supposed to live? I need *money*." I spoke slowly, as if speaking to a child.

"So find another job."

"Easy for you to say. You've got experience. You've got papers. Try being in my position."

"Heaven, you cannot do this job and continue to take your training seriously!" Hiro yelled.

"Then you tell me who's going to pay my rent while I find something else!" I challenged. "Because it's not going to be you!"

"That's not fair, Heaven," Hiro said, his voice deathly calm. "You know I'd help you out if I could."

"Fine. But you can't. So what do you suggest?" Beneath my anger ran a thin thread of fear. In that moment I felt my aloneness acutely. Nobody was looking out for me except myself. That much was clear.

"What happened to the money your father sent you?"

"Not that it's any of your business, but I had to pay a security deposit and first and last month's rent to move in with Cheryl. And the last of it went for groceries and bus fares after I lost the job at Life Bytes. I'm not totally irresponsible, you know."

"I didn't say you were," Hiro said, but he looked doubtful.

"I suppose you could have made the money go much further, hmm?" I sputtered, wanting to just get out of the room, the dojo—away from his disapproval, which hurt me more than he could ever know.

"Possibly, yes," Hiro answered, his face hard.

"Well, I guess I just suck! How about that? Can we at least agree on that?"

"Don't be such a child, Heaven," Hiro said with an exasperated sigh. "This isn't about you 'sucking.' I think you just need to be a little more independent. Just because you got offered one job doesn't mean you have to take it. You need to take the initiative and find something that works for you."

"Are you kidding?" I wanted to wring his neck. "I *have* a job! I told you that! I got it for myself, and I don't remember asking you or anyone else for help!" *No need to tell him it was Cheryl who got me the job,* I thought. *The point is, it wasn't him.*

Hiro closed his eyes for moment, and I stood there, trembling with anger, waiting for him to speak. I resisted the urge to make a break for it while he still had his eyes closed. After thirty seconds or so he opened them.

"I think your anger is misplaced. You're taking your frustrations about your situation out on me. Maybe you need to find some people your own age to spend time with. People who share your interests. People who can help you get some good work. Some friends of Cheryl's, maybe?"

I felt like I had been punched in the gut. Was Hiro, my *only* friend (if you could even call him that, at this point) and the only person who knew what I had been through, actually telling me I needed to get a life? I stared at him.

"Don't be angry, Heaven," Hiro soothed, taking a step toward me. "I'm trying to understand your anger. But I don't think I'm the one who can help you with it. I think we need a break."

Ha! I thought bitterly, *I think I'm getting dumped without ever having had a boyfriend!*

"A break from training?" I asked quietly, feeling like I was sinking into a bottomless well of loneliness. Tears came to my eyes and I angrily blinked them away.

"Not exactly. More like an agreement that you'll try to spend more time with some other people."

I looked down at the wooden floor of the practice room. Yep. I was being dumped.

"So you're saying you'll be my teacher but not my friend?"

Hiro looked nervous. "Don't make it sound that way. I—"

"Then forget it!" I interrupted, wishing that I could hit him, kick him, do anything to break through his seriousness, his "professionalism." Didn't he remember any of the things we'd been through? The moments we'd shared? It occurred to me that those minutes and hours must have meant nothing to him, and I couldn't bear the hurt of that realization. "I quit!" I yelled, overcome with the desire to hurt him. "How's that? I quit my stupid training! Now you don't have to worry about me, or my substandard job, or spending time away from Karen!"

Hiro's face was like stone. "I don't think that's wise," he said icily.

"Well, I'm not a wise girl, am I?" I picked up my backpack and strode out of the room without looking at him again. I felt empty inside—without training, what would I be? And without Hiro, what was there left to hope for? I tried to tell myself that I was finally free, that I could do what I wanted and build a real life for myself—but I didn't believe it. Not really. Hiro couldn't have made it clearer that he didn't have time for me in his Karen-filled life. Well, I wouldn't be a burden to him anymore.

I can take care of myself, I thought as the tears slid down my cheeks.

I wanted to crawl into my bed and sleep forever.

When I woke up this morning, Karen kissed me good-bye, and I felt, for the first time since the kidnapping, that everything was going to be okay. When the Yukemuras took Karen by mistake, I was racked with guilt—not only because caring for me had put Karen in danger, but because a tiny part of me was glad they hadn't taken Heaven. It's a terrible thing to feel that way—and to have to hide it. But I was fairly certain they wouldn't hurt Karen, wouldn't take the risk of involving an innocent American. If they'd caught Heaven, on the other hand—anything could have happened. These yakuza men have no souls. They are cruel and have no respect for life.

Thanks to Heaven's bravery, we got Karen back. I saw her looking so scared and helpless, Karen who is so strong, and for the first time I felt angry at Heaven for bringing her problems to me. I left Japan to get away from all that—and now I've landed right in the middle of somebody else's feud. Karen was understanding, but she made it clear that she wanted a normal relationship. For the last few weeks I've been trying to regain her trust—we've cooked dinners together, gone on walks. Done yoga together at her place . . . and this morning, things did feel normal again.

Until the phone call.

I want to help Heaven. It is my duty, my destiny. I care about her—she has a good heart, a strong soul, but she is young and impetuous. If I tell her about what happened this morning, I'm not sure what she would do. I'm not her father. I don't want to be her father. But I feel the need to protect her—maybe from herself. She needs time to heal from what's happened.

Is it right to keep information from her? Who am I to judge?

Usually when I'm on my bike, everything else fades. My mind clears as I concentrate on getting to my destination as quickly as possible, on dodging cars and buses, choosing this turn or that, calculating my rate of speed to fit in each and every pickup and drop-off. But today I'm distracted. I see Heaven sitting on the floor of the dojo, head in her arms, hopeless. I wanted to wrap her up and cradle her—to be her friend. Was I right to let her walk out that door? Could it be that she's walked out of my life for good?

I feel empty. When I first met Heaven and heard how Ohiko had been killed and how she was in danger, I told her I would help her because I believed it was my duty, my destiny. I still believe that.

So why am I fighting it? Why is the path so cloudy? How can one phone call, one argument, one young woman change everything so quickly?

I wish I could talk to Karen about all this. Once she would have understood, but now everything's different.

My shift is almost over. It has been a very long day.

Hiro

4

"Hey, you," Cheryl said when I wandered out into the kitchen. "That was some disco nap!"

"What time is it?" I asked, my voice rusty.

"Seven o'clock. Dinnertime!"

"I can't believe I slept that long." I leaned on the counter. "Smells good—what is it?"

"Cheryl's famous mac 'n' cheese. Guaranteed to give your tummy a nice booze lining."

"It smells delicious." My stomach grumbled, and I realized I was ravenous. I'd downed a big glass of water and a couple of ibuprofens when I got home and gone straight to bed without eating. After what Hiro'd said to me, I hadn't had much of an appetite. I resolved not to think about our argument just yet.

"I've been thinking about last night all day, Heaven. I

just can't get over how much you rock!" Cheryl stirred the macaroni into the cheese sauce, then glopped it into a baking dish, spilling some of it onto the counter.

"Oh, please. It was nothing. I think it seemed more impressive because you'd had a little too much to drink."

"Well, that's an understatement . . . I was *wasted!*" Cheryl said cheerfully. "But I know what I saw, and it was cool."

"Well, thanks," I said. "Really, it's just a few little things."

"You *have* to show me how you did that. I *so* want to be able to protect myself the way you did last night." Cheryl pulled salad stuff out of the fridge and tossed it onto the counter.

"Here, let me wash the lettuce," I said, trying unsuccessfully to change the subject.

"Seriously. Do you think you could teach me how to do some moves?"

"I'm not good enough to train anyone," I said, ripping off lettuce leaves. "Why don't you just take a self-defense class or something?"

"Why spend the money when I have a badass martial arts diva living in my own house? Come on . . . ," Cheryl wheedled, chopping a tomato with manic glee. "What could it hurt?"

"You know—what happened last night was just luck.

Those guys were drugged up and scared and didn't really know what they were doing. They were practically babies."

"Still," Cheryl said, undeterred, "most people can't do what you did. How did you start training with Hiro, anyway? I mean, what made you decide to do that?"

I turned toward the sink, concentrating on washing each leaf of lettuce thoroughly. I'd known these questions might come up eventually—expected it, even— but I'd hoped somehow that I'd be able to avoid them. What was I supposed to tell her? That I had to learn how to protect myself because someone, somewhere, was determined to kill everyone in my family? That I'd been the victim of two ninja attacks already and now it looked like I was up against the Japanese mafia? Telling Cheryl would just put her in more danger than she probably was already just for being my friend. I turned around.

"Cheryl—I'm sorry. I just really can't talk about that. It's not that I don't want to, it's just . . . I'm sorry," I repeated softly. Cheryl's smile faded. I could tell she was hurt. The loneliness I'd felt earlier that day came flooding back. No matter how much I wanted to reach out, I couldn't. Just being who I was put an unbridgeable distance between me and anyone I cared about.

"Why can't you? Don't you trust me?" Cheryl asked, still joking around.

"Of course I trust you." I smiled. "It's not that."

"Then what? Your secrets can't be that deep and dark. Besides, I've told *you* lots of things."

It was true. Cheryl was the kind of person who was into total disclosure. If she liked you, she'd tell you all her most private secrets.

"I know you have. And if they were just my secrets, you know I'd tell you. But this one—I just can't. Please understand," I pleaded, wanting so bad to just tell her the whole story. But I couldn't.

"Okay, whatever," she said quietly, going back to her chopping. "That's fine."

But it wasn't fine. I could tell.

"So why don't you tell me more about Marcus?" I asked, hoping to smooth things over.

"He was nice," Cheryl said without enthusiasm, "whatever." She was definitely hurt. But what could I do?

"I'd tell you if I could," I said softly. "Please believe me."

Cheryl was quiet for a moment, then let out a sigh. "Okay. I just really wish you trusted me."

"Cheryl! I do trust you!" I threw my arms around her. "I trust you *tons.*"

"Ouch! You're going to get stabbed next time you do that," Cheryl said, trying to be funny. But I wasn't so sure she was convinced that my silence had nothing to do with her.

"So . . . are you going to see Marcus again?" I pressed,

trying to break the ice and steer us back to regular conversation.

"Mayyyybe . . . ," Cheryl said, her voice growing warmer. I knew she couldn't stay mad for long.

"Why don't you come with me to Vibe tonight?" I asked hopefully. "Will he be there?" I really *did* want Cheryl to come—suddenly it seemed kind of daunting to be going back there on my own, even though I knew it was a great job.

"He might—but I can't go out. I have an early shift tomorrow, and I barely made it through today without falling over. Maybe tomorrow night."

"Cool," I said. Cheryl and I chatted about Marcus while we finished prepping dinner, and for the moment things felt homey and comfortable. It was nice to be there in the warm kitchen, making some American food and knowing that I was about to go out and earn some money. One of the best things about being on my own in L.A. was that I was learning how to cook. At home all our meals were cooked for us—and though they were delicious, they'd always catered to my father's tastes—not mine. It was liberating to be able to have comfort food when I wanted it and not have to sit down to a dinner of Japanese haute cuisine or a cut of meat slathered in a rich French sauce. Although come to think of it, I'd been craving some yaki-udon lately—stir-fried noodles. Now that I'd have more money and time (I pushed the thought of my argument with Hiro out of my head), I could go shopping in Little Tokyo and buy what I needed to cook some traditional Japanese recipes. I'd have to get a cookbook, though. Pathetically enough, I'd never cooked anything but microwave popcorn until Hiro took me in.

Cheryl and I brought our plates over to the coffee table. Just as I was about to dig in, Cheryl jumped up.

"I almost forgot! Look what I picked up for you." Cheryl dug through her bag and took out two DVDs. "Check it out."

"*Fear of a Black Hat* and *8 Mile*," I read out loud.

"So you can get up to speed on your hip-hop knowledge. *Fear of a Black Hat* is old school—and I'm sure you've heard about *8 Mile*. Eminem is still, like, everywhere. I can't tell if I like him or I hate him." Cheryl looked pensive.

I stared at the movies, feeling guiltier than ever that I couldn't be honest with Cheryl. "That's the nicest thing . . . ," I said. I wasn't used to people going out of their way for me because they wanted—and not because my father was paying them to do it.

"You can watch them whenever. I'm actually kind of surprised you haven't seen them, Miss Movie Buff."

"I wanted to see *8 Mile,* but my father wouldn't let me. I'll definitely check them out soon."

"So what are you going to wear tonight?" Cheryl asked through a mouthful of mac 'n' cheese.

"I don't know. Any suggestions?" I hadn't even thought

about what to wear to Vibe. I didn't have that many options. I'd picked up some new clothes with the money my father sent me before he was attacked, but my wardrobe was still pretty slim.

"Any suggestions? Are you kidding? We'll get you *all* tricked out! Never fear, Cheryl is here!"

I grinned. I couldn't wait to get back to Vibe. And that mac 'n' cheese sure tasted good.

At ten on the dot I found myself in front of Vibe. There was already a line, but I went right up to the velvet rope. The bouncer greeted me with a smile, opened the door, and waved me in.

"I'm Heaven," I said, with an awkward little wave.

"I know. And you are *heavenly*, my dear. I'm Matt."

Matt had been so sweet that I forgave the pun. At least *someone* seemed to approve of me. As I walked down the darkened staircase into the quiet club (it didn't officially open until eleven), I took deep breaths and tried to relax. I was nervous as hell. Without Cheryl around to help me out, I felt every inch the new kid in school.

A. J., the bartender, was lining up glasses behind the bar and talking to a tall guy with cornrows who sat on one of the bar stools nursing a beer. A. J. looked up as I approached and flashed a smile.

"Hey, Heaven, what's up? Good to see you."

"Hey," I said, feeling only slightly less nervous. "How's it going?"

"Good, good. You look great."

"Thanks," I said, a little embarrassed. "I wasn't exactly sure what to wear." With Cheryl's help I'd slithered into a tiny black cocktail dress with a deep cowl neck. She'd parted my hair into sections and twisted each one back and pinned it up. I felt a little naked, but I had to admit—I looked *good*. My motorcycle boots completed the outfit, much to Cheryl's dismay.

"Well, you chose right," A. J. said. "Heaven, meet DJ Slavo—he's going to be spinning for us tonight. Straight from London!"

"Really?" I said, shaking DJ Slavo's hand. "I love London!" I'd always been a little bit of an Anglophile— *Hello!* was one of my favorite tabloids. Or maybe it was just the Cadbury chocolate that had won me over.

"You've been?" he asked, in a surprisingly high and lilting voice. I couldn't quite place his accent. He didn't smile, just fixed me in a hazel-eyed stare. Suddenly I felt like my exclamation had been impossibly stupid.

"Oh, sure," I said, trying to sound less enthused and more chill. "I used to go with my family. I grew up in Tokyo and—" I stopped, horrified. Something about Vibe made it easy to forget that the less people knew about me, the better off I was. *You're just being paranoid, Heaven,* I told myself, but for a second I was frozen. I didn't know how much to say.

"And . . . ?" DJ Slavo said, raising his eyebrows. He looked like he didn't believe me.

"And . . . w-well, nothing," I stammered, trying to recover. *Stupid Heaven!* "London's a great city, but I never really got a chance to go to any clubs there."

"I only recently moved there myself," DJ Slavo said, still looking at me like I was some sort of alien. "I'm from Senegal originally." His voice was mesmerizing—so distinctive. I smiled tentatively at him, blushing. He probably thought I was a huge dork.

I perched awkwardly on a stool and sat quietly as A. J. and DJ Slavo continued their conversation, afraid I'd blurt out something else inane if I tried to chime in. They mentioned people I'd never heard of, with names like Fab Five Freddy and Afrika Bambaataa. It was fascinating just listening to them, really. It made me think about how starved I'd been for any kind of learning—back in Tokyo, learning was my full-time job. I studied all day with tutors and alone, learning all the things my father thought fitting for the daughter of a proud samurai family. Back then, I'd hated him for making me work so hard, but now that I wasn't doing it anymore, I kind of missed it.

"Did you ever check out the hip-hop scene in Tokyo?" A. J. asked. His brown eyes twinkled as he lit a row of candles along the bar. He looked a little bit out of place at Vibe, too, which made me feel better. He was tall and thin, with a thick thatch of golden brown hair that stuck out wildly in all directions. If I'd seen him on the street, I'd never have pegged him as a hip-hop kind of guy. But

that's what was so great about Vibe—there was no one
type.

"Not really," I answered, "but I know there were a lot of
hip-hop clubs in the Shibuya district. Japanese rap is a little
funny—over there, if you like hip-hop, you totally embrace
the styles, the music—but something's missing."

"Blackness?" DJ Slavo offered, and laughed.

"Maybe," I said, smiling. "It is pretty funny when you
hear a bunch of Asian kids trying to be all 'down.'"

A. J. sighed. "It's so weird how that happens—people
are always trying to be the 'other.'"

"Yeah," DJ Slavo said, "but there's actually some interesting stuff coming out of Tokyo right now. You've obviously
heard 'Heaven's Gone,' right?"

My stomach dropped. "What?"

"You know, that Funkitout song—about a girl named
Heaven?" DJ Slavo looked skeptical again. Did he think I
was lying?

I shook my head. This was *really* bad news.

"Oh—I just assumed you'd heard it—maybe even took
the name 'Heaven' from it." DJ Slavo studied my face as he
gulped at his beer.

"Heaven's my real name," I said quietly, feeling the
blood rush from my face. I could only hope that the song
wasn't actually about me. But back when I was in all the
papers after the plane crash, people had made up songs
about my story . . .

"I have a bootleg of it. I can burn a copy for you if you want."

"That'd be great," I said. "I'd like to hear it." What else could this day throw at me? I wondered.

"But you have to promise to translate it for us, too," A. J. said. "I've heard it a few times and I'm dying to know what the lyrics mean."

"No problem," I said, hoping it wouldn't be.

"Well, I'd better get ready." DJ Slavo headed back to the corner of the club where his tables were set up. A. J. looked at his watch.

"Oh God—it's almost eleven. Where's Nina?"

"Nina?"

"She's one of the other bartenders."

As if on cue, Nina came running down the steps. She was the model type I'd seen behind the bar the night before.

"Sorry, A. J., sorry!" Nina gasped, throwing her leather jacket off to reveal a minuscule halter top that hung perfectly off her graceful frame. Pure *Vogue*.

"Nina—you've been late every night this week!"

I stared at Nina as she and A. J. spatted over her start time. She had to be at *least* six feet tall in her heels, and with her dark skin and shaved head she was beyond runway—she was supermodel. Huge hoops dangled from her ears, and a necklace made of dark red shiny beads nestled on her collarbone.

"Who's this?" Nina asked, looking me up and down. I stood up from the stool.

"I'm Heaven," I said, holding out my hand.

Nina offered me a limp hand, then jerked it away with barely a touch. My palms *were* a little sweaty, but it was still kind of rude, I thought.

"Heaven's gonna be the new shot girl," A. J. said.

Nina stared at me. "Just remember—if *I'm* making the shots, *you're* splittin' the tips."

I looked at A. J. He rolled his eyes.

"I'll be making Heaven's shots until she learns how to do it, Nina. Don't worry. And she'll be keeping her tips."

"Whatever you say," Nina huffed. "I've got to go fix my face." She flounced off to the bathroom.

"She's amazing looking," I said, feeling suddenly young and exceedingly unglamorous.

"Maybe a little *too* amazing looking." A. J. sighed. "She's got some modeling stuff going on, so she's kind of chronically late. Not to mention that she's a total pain-in-the-ass diva."

"Oh." I'd never met a real live model, though I was anything but surprised. I felt like shrinking another inch or two. With Nina around, why did they need *me?*

"Anyway," A. J. continued, "she draws the guys in. They love her. Don't let anything she says get to you. Listen—if you're late, by the way, just give a call and let me know. That's one of the only rules around here."

"Cool. What can I do?" Might as well make myself useful.

"Well, first I need to show you how to make some shots. We've got a few minutes before Matt opens the doors, and no one really starts showing up until midnight, anyway. I'll teach you to make a couple of kinds, but you won't have to make them for yourself until things get busy around one. Before that, just bring your tray over and I'll hand you a fresh one."

A. J. pulled bottles down onto the bar and lined up glasses on a tray. Now that I had something to do, I started to loosen up and enjoy myself. Pouring the liquor into the tiny shot glasses was almost like chemistry or something.

"Here, taste this," A. J. said, holding out a purple concoction.

I sniffed it suspiciously.

"Go on."

I gulped it. Delicious. "It tastes like grape," I said happily.

"It's called a 'purple haze.' Very popular," said A. J., smiling. He pulled out some lemons from behind the bar and went back to work like a mad professor over his test tubes. "And this is a 'lemon drop.' Vodka, lemon juice, and sugar. Simple, yet delicious."

I picked up one glass and A. J. another.

"Cheers," he said, and we drank.

"Ooh." I squinted, making a face. "Sweet and sour." I laughed. DJ Slavo was spinning now, and I was starting to think this job might actually turn out to be as fun as I'd imagined. A. J. filled up the remaining glasses and handed me a wad of cash.

"All right, killer," A. J. joked, "get out there and do your thing."

I took a deep breath and grabbed the tray, surprised to find that I was so tense, my knees were shaking. I felt obvious with only a few people in the bar. It seemed so daunting to have to go talk to all these strangers, and I hardly knew what to say. I tried to think of how the waiters had acted at all the parties my father had thrown or the engagement parties I'd had to attend with the Yukemuras before I left Japan. They never really said much, although in retrospect I guess they did look a little scared. I adjusted my face into what I hoped was a pleasant, competent look and approached a table of three guys. They were deep in conversation, and I wasn't sure if I should interrupt.

"Would you like a shot?" I squeaked. They kept talking. I cleared my throat and repeated the question, but it came out way too loud. The guys looked at me strangely.

"What?" said the one in the center of the booth. He seemed like their leader somehow.

"Shot?" I repeated, wanting to sink through the floor.

"What kind are they?"

"Ummm . . . lemon drops," I blurted. "Or purple haze."

"What's in the purple haze?"

My mind went blank. "They taste like grape," I said, kicking myself mentally. What had A. J. said? "Grape shnopes," I said.

"You mean schnapps?" one of the guys said, looking at his friends and grinning.

"Scnappes, that's right." I wanted to sink into the floor. "They're really good," I added pathetically.

"No, thanks," he said, and went back to his conversation.

I walked quickly away from the table, hoping that A. J. hadn't seen. I glanced over at the bar and saw Nina watching me with a smug look on her face. *Stupid Heaven, stupid!* I thought.

Schnapps, *schnapps*, I repeated to myself as I searched for someone who looked nice.

"Hey, you!" Two girls were waving some cash in the air.

"Shot?" I asked, my heart pounding. You'd think I was making a drug deal or something!

"What kind do you have?"

"Lemon drops and purple hazes."

"Ooh, I love lemon drops. Can we have three?"

I tried to maneuver the three shots off the tray and almost dropped the whole thing. "Whoops," I said, laughing nervously. "That'll be fifteen dollars," I said after I finally managed to get the glasses safely onto the table.

One girl handed me a twenty. I groped in my apron for change with one hand while the shots on my tray rattled precariously. I was still fishing for the bills after they'd downed their shots.

"Just keep the change," the girl said, and slid their empties back on my tray.

"Thanks," I said, feeling like a total idiot. Not the smoothest exchange, but I'd made five bucks in less than a minute! I vowed to practice my tray-balancing maneuvers when I got a chance.

The club began to fill, and I soon spotted Dubious, sitting at the same table he'd been at the night before. I decided to be bold. If I was ever going to make enough money to pay back Cheryl *and* support myself, I'd have to start exploiting every possible angle. And as Cheryl said, Dubious would be good practice.

"Hey, Dubious!" I pasted a smile on my face.

"Hey—is it Heaven?"

I nodded.

"Wow—you work here?" Dubious looked so genuinely impressed that I had to feel proud of myself.

"As of tonight," I said. "Would you like to buy some shots?"

"Sure, I'll take one," Dubious said, and handed me a ten. "But what are you going to do for me?" He smiled.

Okay, I thought. *He's flirting.* "Ummm . . . stand here while you drink it?" I asked.

Dubious laughed. "If you give me a kiss, you can keep the change." He stuck a finger in his mouth and gnawed at his nail. Wow. He was really unsmooth. But if it meant another five bucks . . .

"Okay," I said, giving him a quick peck on the cheek, "but don't tell anyone."

Dubious downed his shot with a grin. "Can you sit down and talk for a while?" he asked hopefully.

"Sorry, I can't. But it looks like there are a lot of nice girls here tonight. You should do fine."

Dubious nodded. "Okay. Bye, Heaven."

"Bye." I left Dubious's table feeling slightly more confident. If I could just get to know some regulars, the job would be a lot easier.

"Hey, you! Give me four of those!" I turned around. A hulking man in sunglasses was looming over me. I gulped. This was not exactly what I had expected. I held out my tray, trying not to shake the glasses on it. How was it that I could beat up two muggers and I was scared to death of handing out a few drinks?

"Five each," I said, trying to sound sassy.

He grabbed the glasses off my tray and passed them back to his friends.

"And how much for you?" he said, pinching my butt.

"Not for sale!" I yelled. His friends laughed. I wanted to smash my tray over his head, but I resisted.

Mr. Sunglasses laughed, too. "I'm just kidding, honey,

just kidding." He turned to his friends. "She's a fighter!"

"That's right," I said, finding my confidence again. "Better watch out!"

"Another round from the fighter!" he said, and they gulped down the last of the shots. He dropped a fifty on the tray.

"That's for being so cute," he said, and turned away.

Cheryl would be proud of me. I'd been firm but playful. *Too bad there's no one to share my triumph with,* I thought as I headed back to the bar for a refill. *Just think about the money,* I said to myself, *at twenty bucks a tray, you'll be back on your feet in no time. . . .*

5

By two in the morning Vibe was jam-packed. People seemed to be loving DJ Slavo's grooves, and I bopped from group to group with my tray, which I'd refilled countless times. The wad of cash in my apron pocket was getting huge, and I'd become a lot smoother in my routine. Most of the guys were jerks who didn't seem to really want a shot so much as an easy flirting target. And I'd learned they weren't all such big tippers—they wanted you to work for it. But if I could just put up with a little groping, I'd learned, the rewards were pretty good. *Rent, rent,* I repeated when a customer hassled me to the limits of my patience. I tried not to think about what Hiro would say if he saw me. In fact, I tried not to think about Hiro at all.

I got rid of the last few shots on my tray and headed back to the bar.

That's when it happened.

The laugh. I froze, every fiber in my body brought immediately to attention. I spun around, searching the crowd. Had I really heard that laugh? It could only belong to one person—Teddy Yukemura. Back in the day, Ohiko and I called him "The Hyena." Could it be that he was at Vibe?

There. A head of yellowy, dyed hair. A leather jacket. On the other side of the club. I hadn't heard a word from him since the day he'd called and told me the location Karen's kidnappers had picked for the exchange—information that had allowed Hiro and me to prepare—and probably saved my life. When I'd tried to call Teddy's cell phone after we got Karen back, it had been disconnected. He'd vanished into thin air.

"Hey!" I slammed my tray of empties down on the closest table, ignoring the protests of the people who sat there, and pushed my way across the dance floor, trying desperately to keep the yellow head (Teddy's head?) in view, which was hard in the dim light of the club. I realized how desperately I wanted that yellow head to be his—I'd worried since the exchange that the Yukemuras had done something horrible to him—and all because he'd helped me.

It was weird—a few months ago I'd hated him more than anyone else in the world. But I'd learned that Teddy wasn't exactly the terrible guy I'd thought—like me, he was just a pawn in the dangerous game our families were playing. He'd made mistakes, of course, and hadn't been strong

enough to stand up to his father, but was I any better? My family was tainted, too, and my brother had likely died for refusing to become a yakuza member.

Something that was outside our control had stolen our lives from us—and even if Hiro couldn't understand that, Teddy would.

I wanted it to be him so badly.

"Teddy!" I yelled, but the yellow head didn't turn around. A couple spun in front of me, and when I dodged around them, he was gone. I made for where I had last seen him and whirled around, searching, searching. . . .

There. I leapt forward and grabbed at his leather jacket. "Teddy!" I yelled, ready to throw myself into his arms. He turned . . .

"Nope, sorry. I'm Mike. Wanna dance?" An unfamiliar face—nothing like Teddy's—leered at me. I shuddered. He wasn't even Asian.

"No, thanks. Sorry." I walked slowly back to the table where I'd left my tray, disappointment oozing through me. Why couldn't it have been Teddy? More than anything, I wanted to talk to someone who I didn't have to hide *anything* from. Was that so much to ask?

"Heaven, are you okay?" A. J. asked when I loaded up the tray. "You look a little pale."

"I'm fine," I said, mustering a smile.

"All right, then get back out there!" He pushed a full tray across the bar. "Make some money!"

"Okay," I said, trying to sound perky. I was tired and beaten down, but I couldn't exactly tell A. J. that. I felt stupid for letting myself believe that the guy might have been Teddy. Wishful thinking. Sure, he was into hip-hop, but what were the chances that he'd show up at the very club where I'd *just* started to work?

Right now, an ally like Teddy would be pretty comforting. Hiro wanted to protect me. He had my best interests in mind, but he was too rigid. Everything was black and white for him. But in my life, there were only shades of gray. I thought about our earlier argument and felt suddenly like I might cry. As imperfect and unfulfilling as my relationship with Hiro had been, now—it was over. There was no point dissecting something that didn't exist.

I stepped behind the bar for a glass of water before making the rounds. If only I could forget about everything, make it go away.

"Nice to have a break, huh?" Nina asked, looking over from the cash register.

"Me?" I asked, not sure who she was talking to.

"Yeah, you. Bartenders don't get breaks on a night like this."

"Oh." I couldn't tell what she was getting at. "I just needed some water."

Nina shrugged. "Whatever you say. If I were you, I'd be out there making some money instead of back here making excuses."

"Thanks for the advice," I said as Nina moved back down the bar, "but I think I've got the hang of it." What the hell was her problem?

Nina turned back around. "So you're an expert now, huh?"

I drank the rest of the water and picked up my tray. "I guess I am." I was too deflated to bother being nice to her. If she wanted to play it like that, so be it.

Her eyes shot daggers at me. Did she have something against me? Or was she just generally sort of weird and off-putting? If she hadn't been so drop-dead gorgeous, I would have sworn she was threatened by me. Well, Miss Supermodel had nothing to worry about. I headed back to work. *Great,* I thought, *you've been at Vibe less than a night and you've already made an enemy.*

"Well, if it isn't little Miss Heaven . . ."

I turned at the sound of the familiar voice. Suddenly Marcus stood next to me, smiling at me with that strange, slow smile. He was wearing a red-and-white track suit, which, although it would have looked completely ridiculous on some guys, made him look buff and hot. The jacket was unzipped, revealing a tight tank top that showed off his six-pack. Yellow-tinted sunglasses half hid his eyes.

"Hi," I said, standing up a little straighter and trying to look more like I imagined a confident shot girl just about to head back to the job might look. Why did Marcus make me feel so tense?

"Taking a break?" he asked, squeezing a little closer to me.

"Kind of," I said, then added, "Cheryl couldn't come tonight. She had to be at work early tomorrow."

"Too bad," Marcus said, but he didn't sound too bummed out. "So how's life in these United States treating you?"

"What do you mean?" I asked, tensing even more. Why would he ask me a question like that?

"Well," Marcus drawled, lighting a cigarette, "Cheryl said you'd only been in the States for a few months, and I figured that must be a big change."

"Yeah, I guess. I'm just getting settled in before starting school," I lied, hoping he'd drop the subject. I'd always wanted to go to UCLA. It seemed like as good a reason as any for my being in the States.

"School? Now, that's not what I heard."

"What are you talking about?" I snapped, wishing he would just leave me alone. He was giving me the creeps, and I had work to do. I noticed A. J. staring at us from the other side of the bar—Nina stood beside him with a nasty smile on her face—and I inched a little farther away from Marcus. She was probably telling A. J. that I was slacking off or something—what if I lost my job after just one night? I had to get back to work—*now*.

"Not a thing, not a thing," Marcus answered vaguely, "except I heard your agenda might be a little different." He looked me in the eye. I wished he'd take off those sunglasses.

"What did Cheryl tell you?" I asked, my voice harsh. "I don't know what you're getting at."

"Whoa, chill out, girl," Marcus drawled, and put a hand on my shoulder. "I'm just saying you got yourself a job here, and maybe a few friends, and maybe school isn't your priority right now." He massaged my shoulder with strong fingers. A chill ran through me. Something definitely was not right with him. And I had the sickening feeling he might be hitting on me.

"Maybe," I answered shortly, jerking my shoulder away. "I really don't know. I've got to get back to work." I tried to get A. J.'s attention.

"Why you have to be like that?" Marcus asked, grabbing my wrist. He wasn't the gentle player anymore. "I think you *do* know. You just don't want to tell Marcus."

"P-Please," I stammered, trying to get my wrist back without dropping the tray I'd picked up.

"Please what?" Marcus hissed, leaning over so that his face was close to mine.

"Everything okay here?" A. J. said. I breathed with relief.

"Hello, my brother," Marcus said, dropping my wrist as though surprised to find he'd been holding it at all. A. J. glanced at me with what looked like concern.

"See you guys later," I mumbled, and escaped back into the crowd. As I turned from the bar, I noticed that Nina was staring at A. J. with a weird look on her face. Clearly some kind of Vibe drama was going on, and I wasn't exactly sure what it was. I felt almost as alien as when I'd washed up at Cheryl's party that first night of the wedding, unsure of what to do or say and without any clue as to how to read a social situation. When I was sure no one was looking, I downed one of my shots. I figured, hey, that's what people do in the movies when they're freaked out, right? My head was spinning and my nerves were frayed. I didn't know what to think. One thing I knew for sure—Cheryl needed to stay away from Marcus. He was extremely sketchy.

By the time Vibe cleared out, it was four in the morning. I'd given A. J. my heap of cash, and now he was laying out my tips on the bar.

"Two-twenty, two-thirty, two-forty . . . ," he counted, "two fifty-five. And some change. You did great."

"Wow," I said, collecting the bills from the counter, "that's half my rent right there." If I hadn't been so utterly drained, I would have jumped up and down with joy. It was the most money I'd *ever* made on my own. And I'd made it all by myself.

"Just don't spend it all in one place." I nodded, hardly able to muster up a laugh. My feet were killing me, and I could have fallen asleep right then and there. But it was worth it. I'd be able to pay Cheryl back in no time!

"Well, well, well, looks can be deceiving," Nina commented as she walked by behind the bar.

"What's that supposed to mean?" I asked, wanting to strangle her.

"Nothing," she said lazily, a nasty smile playing at the corners of her mouth, "just who'd have thought *you'd* rake it in like that?"

I stared at her with what I hoped was disdain but said nothing. *No sense in starting trouble,* I told myself. *Just let it go.*

"Nina, why don't you finish cleaning the glasses?" A. J. asked, looking annoyed. Nina bowed sarcastically and went to the other end of the bar to finish her closing duties. "Sorry about that," A. J. said. "She's very territorial."

"So I see."

"Don't let it bother you," A. J. said. "You did a fantastic job. Really."

"Thanks," I said, trying to let go of Nina's snottiness. I yawned. "I think I have to get used to this late schedule." I felt fuzzy and buzzed and couldn't wait to get home. I drank down the rest of the vodka cranberry A. J. had made for me before he counted out my tips. It felt so adult to be coming off a shift and having a nightcap. And even if Nina was a bitch, A. J. was nice.

"It does take some adjusting to," A. J. commiserated. "But you'll get into the groove. Do you want me to call you a cab?"

I nodded. "Thanks." I wasn't about to risk a mugging with all that cash on me. And for the first time I had plenty of money to pay for it.

After A. J. and I worked out my schedule for the coming week, I climbed wearily up the steps, almost bumping into Matt, the bouncer, who was on his way down.

"You got a ride home?" he asked.

"A. J. called me a cab."

"Good. Be careful."

Nice to know someone *cares,* I thought.

I pushed open the heavy door and stepped into the deserted street. The taxi was nowhere in sight. I leaned back against the wall of the building, closed my eyes, and slowly rubbed my temples. My mind was cluttered, and I couldn't tell if the feeling of unease I had was just a result of one vodka cranberry too many or—something else. Had Marcus really been weird, or was I just rattled from the potential Teddy sighting? Had I really seen Teddy? Nothing that had happened to me all night seemed to make any sense.

I opened my eyes. Still no cab. I wondered if the driver might have trouble finding Peabody, which was more of an alley than a street, really, and decided to walk up to the intersection. My boots clopped loudly on the pavement. I shivered, vowing to bring a pair of jeans to change into the next time I worked.

Ten minutes. Fifteen. Still no cab. I thought about going back to Vibe, but it seemed quicker just to head for the bus stop. After a few blocks I heard the engine of a car behind me, and I turned around, expecting to see a taxi.

It wasn't a taxi.

A Mercedes with tinted windows came down the street toward me. I walked faster, praying that it would drive right past me.

The Mercedes slowed to a crawl. One of its tinted windows rolled down with a faint buzz.

Yakuza. I recognized the thuggish face of one of the men who'd kidnapped Karen. That meant they were working for the Yukemuras. I broke into a sprint. How had they found me? Had they been trailing me this whole time, just waiting for a second chance to strike?

"Get her!" I heard him shout in Japanese as I scooted onto a side street. The car squealed into action behind me, and I heard the sound of a door slamming, followed by feet hitting the pavement.

They were gaining on me. There was no way to outrun them. I'd have to fight.

I stopped short, tripping the goon who was closest to me before he even had time to register that I'd stopped running. He went sprawling onto the sidewalk. I crouched as the others approached, trying desperately to work out some sort of plan, but my brain was stuck on repeat. All I could think about was the window of the car sliding down and the thug's leering face. I tried desperately to focus.

There were three of them besides the one I'd already dropped. I'd fought more, but not in this condition. I let my punches fly as they closed in, feeling the gratifying thud of my fist connecting with a jawbone, a kidney, a gut, before a splinter of pain ripped through my side. I'd taken a sharp kick to my side, and the force of it propelled me back. I'd let down my guard—sloppy. With a grunt I hurled myself back into the melee, whirling among my attackers like a pinball, lashing out, landing a few hits, but nothing powerful enough to stop them.

Just as I realized that all the booze I'd drunk had clouded my ability—I was in essence fighting blind, unable to predict their next moves—two muscled arms closed around my waist. My feet left the ground and I was slammed back down to the pavement hard enough to knock the wind out of me. Sidewalk guy had come back into the fray. I strained for breath and struggled as he held me down.

"Shou ga nai," my old friend the kidnapper hissed, his face close to mine, his breath reeking of garlic and stale smoke. "There's no help for it—we'll have to kill you now."

In a rush my wind suddenly came back. I screamed as loud as I could. He clamped his hand down on my mouth and nose, and I panicked, straining for just one more breath.

Could this be how it was going to end? Alone, still not knowing who had killed my brother, in some dark, dank alley in downtown L.A.? I regretted quitting my training with every fiber of my being—and now Hiro would never know how much I'd cared about him. . . .

Suddenly a siren broke the silence of the street. The goon took his hand off my mouth and I rolled onto my side, first retching, then sucking in the air in huge delicious mouthfuls.

"Keikan!" someone yelled. "Police!" As if in a dream, I heard them deciding what to do with me.

"Get her in the car!" said their leader.

"There's no time! The cops are here!" replied another.

"Dammit!" Through a haze I saw the approaching lights of the police cruiser. My attackers jumped into the Mercedes and sped away. I hauled myself off the sidewalk. I couldn't let the police find me. I'd have to answer questions I wasn't ready to answer. Grasping my side, I slid around the corner and ducked down behind a Dumpster, trying to make my breathing slow and regular.

The cruiser drove by without stopping. I was safe.

Safe. Ha! I let out a bitter laugh.

After a few minutes I stood up, assessing my injuries. My throat hurt, and so did my side, but nothing felt broken. I'd taken the worst kick below the ribs—it would make a stunning bruise, but nothing more. I waited a few more minutes, then cautiously slid back out onto the street.

And wouldn't you know it? A taxi was driving toward me, as calm as you please. Luck came at a high price these days, it seemed.

I hailed it, crawled in, then burst into tears.

"You okay, honey?" the driver asked, checking me out in his rearview mirror. "Boy trouble?"

"Just take me home," I sniveled, "Ten-ten Dawson Street." Boy trouble. That was a laugh. Though I guess, in a way, it was true. My father, Teddy's father, Teddy—all the ninjas and thugs in between—Hiro—they were all boys, and the trouble was nowhere near ending.

I sobbed halfway home but stopped as the cab climbed the final hill up toward Dawson. The sun was coming up over L.A., over the lush yards and gated houses of the wealthy, over the Hollywood sign. I wiped my eyes with the hem of my dress and sighed. My silly dreams of a "normal" life were just that. There was no avoiding it—they would keep coming after me until I was dead or until I found out what they were after and got to them first. No time for tears and self-pity.

Remember Ohiko, I whispered to myself as the cab climbed higher and the dawn grew brighter over the dirty, sleeping city, *because his memory is all you have left.*

How sweet it is to be back with my homies. Things were touch and go there for a while. I thought I might go crazy locked up in that dark little room, nothing but the drip, drip of water and that rustling, nibbling sound to keep me company. I waited there for what seemed like an eternity.

They knew I'd helped Heaven. But they didn't know why.

When I heard Gojo's voice saying, "Yo, Teddy, what's up, dog? You okay?" I thought I was gonna start crying like a little baby. Lying there on the slab with my eyes covered and my hands and feet tied, I'd been through just about every wack-ass scenario in my head. The yakuza don't dig it when one of them goes off track, know what I'm saying?

"Gojo? Gojo, man, you gotta get me out of here."

"What do you think I'm here for, man? Just shut up."

Gojo risked his life to save me. Pretty unexpected for a brother whose idea of action is two or three hours playing Grand Theft Auto: Vice City. But I guess all that PlayStation taught him a thing or two because he had the car waiting and everything.

"Your pops is mad pissed," Gojo said as we jumped in his SUV and hit the road. I felt like my eyes were gonna explode out of my head from the sunlight. "Damn, dog, you ripe," Gojo said, waving his hand in front of his face. "Roll down that window."

I'd put Gojo in his place later. What did he expect? Not like he would be smelling like a player after a week tied up in a room.

"What did he say?" I asked.

"Who?"

"My father, stupid. Who do you think?"

"I don't know, man, but word on the street was that he was going to leave you there until you was half dead or something. Or maybe all the way dead."

"How'd you know where I was?"

"We followed some of your dad's boys."

I was silent. Gojo must have known that busting me out of that hellhole could get him killed.

"You did that for me?" I whispered, wanting to cry again like a damn baby.

"Yeah, man, but you gotta make it good with your pops. Or we're all screwed."

I nodded. "Take me where I can get cleaned up."

Gojo drove back to his place. I stared out the window, watching the girls on the street. Every time we passed one with long dark hair, I thought of Heaven. Back in that room, the thought of her was all I had. I imagined what it would have been like if we had gotten married after all. Would have been pretty cool.

Gojo was right. I'd have to make it right with my father. But where did that leave Heaven?

Teddy

6

Just please don't let Karen be here, I prayed as I rang Hiro's doorbell. I'd slept until two, then come over to Hiro's before I could change my mind. Only when I was standing at his door did it occur to me that maybe I should have called first. It was the first time I'd been back to the house on Lily Place since the night Karen was kidnapped. I missed the little bungalow where Hiro and I had first gotten to know each other. Once the house was a safe haven—but not anymore. They—whoever *they* were—knew that Hiro was helping me. And they knew where he lived.

"Heaven? What a surprise!"

Karen.

"Oh, h-hey," I stammered, "how are you? I just, um, I just came by to talk to Hiro about something."

"Everything's okay, isn't it?" Karen asked, leaning up

against the door frame. She was wearing the bottom half of the gi, which was a pair of white cotton drawstring pants, and a sports bra. Her bod looked so *healthy*—I pictured the dark purple bruise that had greeted me this morning when I woke up and hobbled painfully to the bathroom. You would have never guessed that just a few weeks ago, she'd been kidnapped and tied up with no food or water in a room for days. Could *anything* make her look bad?

"Heaven?" Karen asked, waving her hand in front of my face. "You okay?"

"Pretty much," I said, trying to look past her without being obvious. She certainly didn't seem too eager to ask me in. "Is Hiro here?"

"Yes, he's here—Hiro!" Karen called back over her shoulder. "Heaven's here to see you!" Karen remained at her post, making me feel even more like an intruder than I already did. "You look a little tired, Heaven. Must be those late nights at the club?" Her voice was thick with disapproval—and a healthy dose of condescension.

"I'm still getting used to it." I wanted to tell her to shut up and leave me alone, but that didn't seem like the right approach somehow.

Hiro walked over toward the door, pulling on a T-shirt. "Heaven? What are you doing out there? Come in." Seeing him made me want to cry with relief. I needed him too much to stay mad at him. I *cared* about him too much. And when he looked at me, it was impossible to believe that he'd really meant what he said yesterday about needing a break from me.

Karen moved out of my way, *finally,* and I stepped into the foyer.

"I'm sorry to bother you, Hiro, but I need to talk to you for a second." I glanced over at Karen, hoping she'd take the hint that I wanted our conversation to be private.

"Don't be silly—it's no problem. Let's go into the kitchen." Hiro turned toward Karen, who was still standing guard like a watchdog. What was her *problem?* Did she think I was going to slam Hiro down on the ground and make out with him? "Are you leaving for the dojo now, sweet?" Hiro asked Karen.

Gross.

"Yep. I'll see you over there later." Karen walked over to Hiro and gave him a long, slow kiss. Very showy. Hiro shot me an embarrassed look and patted Karen awkwardly on the shoulder.

"Okay, bye."

Karen looked at me with—was that triumph on her face? It was ridiculous. What did she have to be jealous about? Obviously Hiro wanted to be with her. What guy wouldn't? *Just go ahead and kick me while I'm down, why don't you?*

Hiro brewed some tea, and I sat down at the table. It was just like the old days, but I felt about a million light-years

95

away from the scared, trusting girl I'd been when I lived here. Now it felt even *more* awkward being there with him alone. There was something between us now, something uncomfortable and unsaid.

"Hiro," I started, "I'm sorry about what happened yesterday. I want to train with you again. I made a mistake."

Hiro sat down. One look into his eyes told me that he wasn't mad anymore, and my anxiety evaporated. I hadn't even realized how worried I'd been that he'd refuse to take me back.

"What changed your mind?"

I told him about last night's attack and about how I had flubbed the fight. I even told him about the drinks I'd had, figuring that total honesty was the best policy. When I finished my story, Hiro's face was strained.

"You're sure they were yakuza?"

"Positive. That beefy, fat-faced guy who kidnapped Karen was there. I saw him before the fight started. And I think the others might have looked a little familiar, too."

Hiro ran his fingers through his hair. "This is not good. I thought the Yukemuras were going to give it a rest."

"You know, Hiro, we can't be positive it's them. I mean . . ." My voice seemed to fail me as I forced out the last part of my sentence. "There are Konishi's yakuza connections to consider. And Teddy's still missing in action."

Hiro nodded. "You're right. But you recognized the ring-leader, and it's unlikely he'd be leading an unrelated crew. The yakuza don't work that way."

I sighed. Hiro's words were cold comfort. Every time I thought about my father's crime connections, which I'd only recently learned about, I felt like everything I'd known my whole life had been a lie. If my own *father* was suspect, then anything was possible.

Hiro gently placed his hand on mine. "I'm sorry, Heaven."

I started to sweat—his hand was warm, and I was worried that nervousness would make me jerk my hand away or throw myself into Hiro's arms. It could go either way.

"Why? It never would have happened if I hadn't been such an idiot." *Breathe, Heaven, breathe.*

"You made a few mistakes. Everyone does." Hiro cleared his throat. "But I'm also sorry about what I said yesterday. I didn't mean to hurt you. And I'm sorry because I know how much you would rather be living a 'normal' life. Who wants to have to worry about being attacked every time they leave their home? It's a terrible way to live. But your destiny has found you, and you can't escape it."

I took a deep breath. He hadn't really meant what he'd

said yesterday after all! "I know. I know. That's why I'm here. I want to work on my mission—I need to clear my head, or something bad is going to happen. I feel it."

"What about your job?" Hiro asked, pouring some more hot water into our cups.

"What about it?" I stiffened.

"Well, don't you think it's not the best idea for you to be working there? Putting aside the problems we—we talked about yesterday . . . ," Hiro stammered, then fell silent as he stirred our tea. Was he actually *embarrassed* about the way he had freaked out yesterday? Sorry was one thing, but—it wasn't like him to regret stuff like that. If there was one thing he was serious about (and really, there were oh so many things), it was the bushido.

". . . it just doesn't seem wise for you to be keeping such late hours—and the Yukemuras obviously know that you're working there now—or somewhere around there."

I sighed. "I know. And you're right, Hiro. But I really don't know what else to do. The truth is, I'm a month behind on my rent, and Cheryl's been buying most of the food for the house—paying the bills. I just can't put that on her. And I'm making really good money." I concentrated on the grounds of tea floating in my cup and tried not to cry. Everything I did seemed hopeless.

"I understand, Heaven. But I think I can lend you some money until you're back on your feet."

"No!" I cried, surprising myself. "I just can't let you do that, Hiro. I mean, you hardly have any money, either. It's not like you're letting your parents support you or any-thing. And besides—where can I work that they won't find me? It doesn't really matter where—it's just a question of time."

"I suppose you're right," Hiro said thoughtfully. "Maybe we've been silly by not getting you out of L.A. alto-gether."

What? Leave L.A.? Panic rose in my throat. I couldn't leave L.A. I just couldn't. Putting aside the fact that I would be totally alone without Hiro and Cheryl, I just didn't have the strength to learn a whole new city all over again. I chose to ignore Hiro's suggestion.

"You know, Hiro—you forget that I'm not even really allowed to work in the United States, which makes things a lot harder. I filled out about twenty applications before I stumbled onto that Life Bytes job—not that *that* lasted very long." I chewed my lip, a bad habit I'd developed since the night of the wedding. Mega-stress.

Hiro nodded. "Okay. I see your point. But so far, noth-ing *inside* the club has seemed weird, right?"

I shook my head deliberately, even as I thought about Marcus. I knew that wasn't the kind of weird Hiro was talk-ing about.

"So listen—why don't you keep it up for the rest of the month and try to catch up on your rent situation? We'll train in the afternoons, and in the meantime you need to do two things—okay?"

"I'm listening."

"First—you *have* to get a ride home *every* night—from the door of the club, okay? Don't you budge from—what's it called? Vibe?—okay, don't budge from Vibe until that taxi is *there*. Make someone wait with you."

I nodded. "No problem. There's a bouncer there, Matt. I'll call the cab before he leaves for the night. And the second?"

"The second is that you have to start looking for another job."

I sighed. "Okay." So much for Heaven's cool new lifestyle. I'd probably be cleaning houses pretty soon. Oh, well.

"Actually—there's a three, too." Hiro leaned forward across the table, his beautiful arms crossed. "I want you to seriously devote yourself to your mission. You *must* clear your mind. That means no drinking."

"That's four, Hiro." I smiled, glad the coziness between us seemed to have returned but not quite sure about this last requirement. "None at all? It might seem kind of weird to have a shot girl who doesn't drink."

"I'm serious. None."

I looked down at my hands. I knew Hiro was right. It wasn't safe for me to drink. I needed to be alert and prepared for anything at any time. I just hoped Cheryl and A. J.

wouldn't ask too many questions about why I wasn't partying. "Okay. No booze."

"Good. Why don't we get back to training right now? You can meet me over at the dojo." Hiro collected our teacups and went over to the sink. I watched his graceful movements and couldn't help wondering why he wasn't in love with me. I mean, I could think of lots of reasons (Karen = hot, Karen = perfect, Karen = way more together than me), but none of them seemed like enough when I compared them to how much I wanted to be with Hiro. It just seemed impossible that someone I loved so much wouldn't love me back. It hurt my heart—a dull, steady ache.

"Okay," I answered, and pushed back my chair. What felt like needles ripped unexpectedly through my side, and before I could hold it back, a small yelp of pain escaped me.

"What's wrong?" Hiro put his arm on my back as I leaned on the chair, trying to breathe through the hurt.

"I'm fine," I said, trying to sound normal, my eyes watering from the effort of fighting the ache in my side. "I just have a little bruise."

"Let me see," Hiro said, sounding every inch the doctor.

"No, Hiro—it's fine, really. . . ."

"Now." I knew better than to argue. I lifted my T-shirt and watched Hiro's face harden. I had to admit, it felt good to have someone caring about what happened to me.

"They did this to you?" he asked, his jaw tightening.

"It's not that bad, Hiro," I said. "I mean, nothing's broken." I looked down at my bruise. It had gone an even deeper shade of blue-purple. But Hiro'd seen me in worse shape.

"Let me get something for that." Hiro rifled through the kitchen drawers, pulling out stacks of herbs to form a hot compress. "What are you doing?" he asked, seeing me still leaning on the chair. "Go lie down on the couch."

I hobbled into the living room, and Hiro followed a few minutes later with the compress. He knelt at my side and rubbed some kind of cream into my bruise, then placed the compress over it. It smelled minty.

"What's in that?" I asked, staring at his beautiful face.

"A bunch of stuff," Hiro said gently. "Mint, aloe . . . different herbs. It's more effective if you can get it on the point of contact earlier, but this should ease the pain enough to make you more comfortable."

"I am comfortable," I said, my eyes feeling heavy. I wanted to stay on that couch forever, with Hiro's hands on my side, his face next to mine, taking care of me. Just the two of us. Maybe I could learn to be happy with what Hiro had to give me. Maybe in time he'd see . . .

"Actually, Heaven, there's something I have to tell you. Something I've been keeping from you." Hiro shifted his hold on the compress, and I opened my eyes. Now I didn't feel tired at all.

"Yes?" My voice trembled. Two competing Heavens were clamoring for attention in my brain. The first said, *He's going to say it—he's going to tell you how he's attracted to you, but he feels like he can't leave Karen right now because of everything that's happened.* The second chastised, *Don't be an idiot—this isn't about Hiro's* supposed *feelings for you. We've been there before.*

Hiro sat down next to me. Was he actually nervous? Was he blushing? Heaven number one was chattering incessantly now—*He's going to tell you! He's going to tell you he loves you!*

"It's hard for me to tell you this. . . ."

I tried to look sympathetic and helpful, but my hands were shaking. I tilted my head and tried to ignore the voice that screamed, *This is it this is it this is it!*

"A few days ago I got a phone call." Hiro cleared his throat.

What? It took my brain a few seconds to process that sentence. What did this have to do with our relationship?

"It was Mieko."

"*Mieko?*" I gasped, trying to sit up. "When did this happen?"

"Lie down," Hiro ordered, pushing gently on my shoulder. "Last week."

"And you didn't think that I should *know?* You thought it was okay to keep that from me?" My anger was growing, and even though part of me sensed it was fueled by disappointment at Hiro's "revelation," I couldn't control it.

"I know, Heaven. I just—I wanted to protect you, and I wasn't sure how to do it. I needed time to think. Eventually I realized I was wrong—"

"You bet you were."

"—and so I'm telling you now. I'm sorry. It was dishonest of me."

"How did she get your number?" I asked coldly.

"She said she got it from Konishi's cell phone." A month after fleeing the wedding, I'd called my father from Hiro's phone to arrange a meeting. A mistake. "Is he still in a coma?" I asked, annoyed that I had to ask Hiro for information about my own family.

"Yes. No change. I'm so sorry, Heaven. I know you loved him." I'd never heard Hiro sound like that. Guess he wasn't as used to screwing up as I was.

"Why are you using the past tense?" I yelled. "He's not dead!"

"I know, I . . ." Hiro looked pained.

"Forget it," I snapped. "I can't believe you. All your talk about *honesty* and the *samurai code*—what a laugh. I can't believe my mother called and you didn't think that was something I needed to know! It's unbelievable!"

"Heaven, you know you've been impetuous in these situations before—I just thought that you should consider it carefully before you contact your family."

"No—you thought *you* should consider it! I'm not a baby, Hiro! I'm sick and tired of you trying to make decisions for me!" I sat up.

"Please lie down, Heaven." Hiro put his hand on my shoulder, and I shook it off. It was a little late for another intimate moment.

"Forget it! I'm fine." I threw the compress on the floor. He was lucky I hadn't chucked it at his head.

Hiro's mouth pursed, and he straightened up. "Look, Heaven—I said I was sorry. And I am. But you're the one who came here asking me to solve your problems, so don't pretend that I'm the one treating you like a child. Take some responsibility for yourself."

I stood up. That was it.

"You know what, Hiro? You can take your training and shove it." I pulled on my sweatshirt. "Sorry to have been such a *burden* to you. How about this? I'll take full responsibility for myself from now on, okay? You won't have to do a thing because you won't see me."

"Heaven . . ." Hiro's voice was stern—why did he always have to play the father? I didn't need another father. I needed a friend.

"Goodbye, Hiro," I said. "You'll let me know if Mieko calls again, I hope. You have my number."

"Don't you want to know what she said?" Hiro asked as I headed for the door.

I stopped. "Tell me," I said, without turning around.

"She just wanted to talk to you. She said Konishi had mumbled your name."

Tears. I turned quickly toward the door to hide them, leaving without another word. Outside, I stumbled down the stairs, noticing gratefully that the pain in my side really was better from the compress, and made it around the corner before giving in to the crying fit. I sobbed like a baby. Crying was about the only thing I was doing well on a regular basis these days. Maybe Hiro was right—I needed to grow up.

But so did he. I wasn't the only one who'd screwed things up. I was sure as hell *finished* with taking the blame.

I can't help it. I know it's awful.

But I hate her.

She's completely destroying my life. Everything was going so well before she showed up. I loved my job, I was totally content in my apartment—loved Echo Park, was having a great time hanging out with Sami and some of the other girls from the dojo. Then Hiro came along, and our feelings for each other just seemed to blossom so naturally, so beautifully.

We were made for each other. We both love what we do. We are committed to our physical training. He likes to do yoga with me, and he cares about the environment and the world we live in. Whether we're just sitting around reading the Sunday paper or going on a bike ride—we have fun. We're on the same wavelength.

At least we were.

Look at me! I'm cowering in my apartment like a baby! Ever since the day they kidnapped me—right from Hiro's doorstep—nothing has been the same. I was so relieved to see him after the whole ordeal. I thought the nightmare was finally over. Hiro'd already been beaten up by the thugs who were after her, and after the kidnapping, well . . . I thought he'd be infuriated with Heaven for messing up our lives that way. I thought he'd tell her to leave us alone.

But he didn't. He wasn't mad at all. In fact, all he could talk about was how guilty he felt for sending her into the kidnappers' lair on her own to save me!

I finally said, "I'm sorry my being here makes you feel so bad. You could have just left me with them."

That *got his attention. He shut up about Heaven after that, for the most part. But I can tell he's distracted. Before this happened, we'd spend hours fooling around, watching movies. Cooking soup together. Now he wants to be alone. He's meditating a lot.*

So where does that leave me?

It's obvious something between us was broken that day. And it's all Heaven's fault. She needs to find someone besides Hiro to give all her problems to. And if he won't tell her so . . . I will. I refuse to play second fiddle to a manipulative nineteen-year-old girl who got herself mixed up in some bad business.

I may be nice, but I'm no pushover. And if Hiro wants action, well, that's what he's going to get.

Karen

7

By the time A. J. counted out my Thursday night pay, my week's total came to $758.

"Not bad for a week's work, huh?" A. J. asked with a smile.

"Not at all." I grinned. "Where'd Nina go, by the way?"

A. J. looked disgusted. "She had to leave early again. You know, if this keeps up, you may get promoted to bartender. And that's where the *real* money is."

"That would be awesome," I said, avoiding A. J.'s eyes. I wasn't sure I wanted to be a bartender at Vibe—it seemed too . . . permanent or something. (Although not having Nina around would unequivocally rock.) What Hiro had said in our last fight was still with me—maybe Vibe wasn't safe. I didn't want to get too attached. Even though I still wasn't training, it seemed to me like *something* had to give. It was only a matter of time.

I'd decided after leaving Hiro's that I wouldn't try to contact Mieko just yet, even though part of me wanted to reach out to her in spite of our problems in the past. It felt good to know that someone in what was left of my family wanted to find me, but I still wasn't sure if I hadn't called because (*a*) I was still trying to prove to Hiro that I wasn't the impulsive, irresponsible teenager he thought I was or (b) because I really thought it might be wiser to wait. I still wasn't sure about Mieko's role in everything that had happened, and knowing that my father had ties to the yakuza made me wary of further contact. The last two times I'd been with my family, I'd been attacked by ninja, and that made *any* communication too risky. Whatever the reason, I'd made my decision. It just felt safer right now not to have contact with home.

I glanced over at Marcus and Cheryl, who were making out in a corner booth. A. J. had flipped on some overhead lights for cleanup, so I could see them all too well. *Stop looking at them, pervert,* a voice in my head scolded. But it was fascinating. Would I ever get kissed like that? Ever? I couldn't help wondering what Hiro and Karen were doing right now. Probably sleeping. Or reading to each other from the bushido. Hiro could be such an old man.

"She better watch out with him," A. J. said, breaking into my thoughts.

"What do you mean? I thought you and Marcus were friends." I leaned against the bar. Over the past week I'd really come to like A. J. He was a genuinely good-hearted guy, and he was patient with my klutziness. Quite a few of Vibe's shot glasses had met an early death at my hands.

"In this business, Heaven, 'friend' is a term used very loosely. Know what I'm saying?"

"Not really," I admitted, feeling a little nervous. I hated not "getting" things.

A. J. leaned closer to me across the bar. "It's all about favors, Heaven. Who can do what for who—who knows people. Marcus knows everybody—and you don't want to be on his bad side." A. J. raised his eyebrows. "He's got *connections*. You understand?"

I glanced over at Marcus, then back at A. J. I was having a foreign language moment. My English was damn near perfect, but there were still some nuances and lingo that went over my head.

"Um—you mean, he's got a shady business? He's a party promoter, right?"

"Sure. But that's not all he is." A. J. widened his eyes. "You know what I mean?"

I was hopeless. "I'm sorry, but you're going to have to help me out here, A. J. . . ."

"You know he's a banger, right?"

A cartoonish image of Marcus wielding a mallet against some helpless pumpkins popped into my head. That couldn't be right. My face must have looked blank because A. J. quickly added: "A *gang*banger."

"He's a gang member?" I whispered. "You're kidding." I shot another look at Marcus and Cheryl. He certainly didn't look like the gangbangers in the movies. No baggy pants, no bandanna. Marcus's style was more P. Diddy wanna-be than *Boyz 'N the Hood*.

A. J. shook his head. "Nope. It's true. He has his fingers in a lot of pies, and he controls a pretty big crew. And they're not exactly nice boys, if you catch my drift."

My heart sank. How many different kinds of organized crime was I going to have to deal with? And Cheryl—did she know?

"It's cool, Heaven," A. J. said. "Marcus has no beef with you."

"What about Cheryl?" I chewed my lip. A. J. patted my hand.

"I'm sure it's fine. I didn't mean to freak you out. She's just a girl he's seeing—he sees lots of them. He'll go out with her for a while, then move on. The only people who have anything to worry about with Marcus are the people he's in business with, okay?"

"Okay," I said, but I wasn't comforted.

"And hey—keep it on the d.l., okay?" A. J. asked with a look toward the make-out booth.

"Sure," I said, and stood up. That was some lingo I knew—Ohiko and I'd had *a lot* of use for a phrase like that with a father as controlling as Konishi. Besides, sometimes it felt like my whole *life* was on the down low. Regardless, it was time for me to take Cheryl home. I hadn't gotten a chance to talk to her much that night, and I hoped she hadn't overindulged.

"Hey, wait," A. J. said as I walked away from the bar. "Slavo burned me a copy of that hip-hop song he was telling you about. Let me know when you figure out the lyrics."

"Oh," I said, still distracted by A. J.'s revelations. "Thanks. I'll listen to it later." I stuffed the CD into my messenger bag. "See you Saturday."

"Cool."

I walked purposefully over to the table and cleared my throat. Marcus opened his eyes and gently pushed Cheryl away. Her glittery bandeau top was sliding down, and I resisted the urge to yank it up like a mother hen.

"Hey, guys. Cheryl, I think it's time to take off."

Cheryl looked irritated. "How about I catch up with you later?"

"It *is* later."

Cheryl's eyes narrowed. "Heaven—"

"No, baby, that's cool," Marcus said, grabbing Cheryl's chin and turning her face toward his. "I'll catch you later. Call me tomorrow and we'll make a plan." He gave her a long, lingering, kiss, opening his eyes and glancing at me before he broke it. I looked away.

Cheryl sighed. "Um . . . okay. Catch you tomorrow."

Marcus nodded. "Bye-bye, ladies. Be good." A slow-motion smile.

Just before I put my foot on the first step out of Vibe, I glanced back at Marcus. His face had lost the lovey-dovey expression. Something else was in its place. Something that looked a lot like hatred. I shuddered and bounded up the stairs, Cheryl behind me.

"Slow down, Power Puff!" Cheryl yelled.

The cab was waiting at the front door. We hopped in, and I sighed a breath of relief as we pulled away. Things were getting downright wiggy, and I wasn't relishing the thought of having to tell Cheryl what I'd found out about Marcus.

"Wanna go have breakfast?" Cheryl said, leaning her head back on the seat.

"Are you drunk?" I asked, trying to sound like I was kidding around and not nagging.

"Drunk on luuuuv, kiddo." Cheryl laughed. "Believe me, the three drinks I had tonight got sweated out of my body a long time ago. Did you see me tearing up the dance floor?"

"I did. I was jealous. Working is great, but I want to do some dancing one of these nights." I ran my hand over my side, testing the bruise to see how it was feeling. The truth was, it had been a struggle just to do my job the first couple of nights after the attack. But I was healing well now, and the bruise was entering the faded, greenish phase. I'd be in dancing form soon enough.

"So—breakfast?" Cheryl asked again, tipping her head toward me.

"Sounds good." I stifled a yawn. I would have rather gone straight home, but I didn't want to hurt Cheryl's feelings. Ever since I'd refused to let her in on my training, she'd been tiptoeing around me—it was nothing she'd specifically said, but I could feel a tension between us that depressed me. Now that Hiro was out of my life *again,* I couldn't afford to lose my only other friend. *Maybe I should keep my mouth shut about Marcus,* I considered.

Cheryl directed the cabdriver to an all-night diner, and soon we were seated at a fifties-style table in red vinyl chairs with all the other club-goers finishing up their nights. I loved kitschy spots like this one, with the waitresses in little pink uniforms with white aprons and hats and things like "malteds" on the menu. In Tokyo there were a bunch of places that imitated the rock-'n'-roll diner theme, but it wasn't the same. Just being in the States made it feel more authentic.

We ordered tall stacks of pancakes, and I added bacon on the side and a Cherry Coke.

"So what's up with you and Hiro?" Cheryl asked. "You haven't been training the last couple of days."

I sighed. I'd wanted to tell Cheryl about the fight, but I couldn't think of a way to do it without bringing up Mieko.

Cheryl knew I wasn't in touch with my family, but without telling her the whole story, my argument with Hiro would just seem sort of psycho.

"He's busy with Karen," I said, which was true—in a way.

"That sucks." Cheryl looked at me sympathetically. "What about A. J.?"

"A. J.? What about him?"

"I think he's got the hots for you."

"No way," I said. "That's crazy."

"Why? He looks at you all the time! He was telling Marcus just tonight what a great job you were doing and how you're good for business." Cheryl fumbled through her bag, looking for change for the mini-jukebox on our table.

"Did Marcus tell you that?" I asked.

"Yep."

"That's nice." Now I felt really guilty. I wondered again if I should even bring up the whole gangbanger issue. But did it really change anything? Even if Marcus had given me some props, it had nothing to do with Cheryl's right to know about how he spent his time. And what kind of friend would I be if I kept something like that from her?

"So—what do you think?" Cheryl asked, punching numbers into the jukebox.

"What are you putting in?" Time for a subject change.

"Don't avoid the question. Um—Elvis. Should I do 'Love Me Tender' or 'In the Ghetto'?"

"'Love Me Tender.' Seventies Elvis is a little more than I can take."

Cheryl finished with the jukebox, then crossed her arms and stared at me. "It. Is. Time. To. Give. It. Up."

I shook my head. Cheryl was unstoppable. "Okay, okay. I think he's really cute. And nice. But . . ."

"But what? What's the problem?"

"Well, for—for one thing, we work together," I stammered.

Cheryl waved a hand dismissively. "That's crap. I've gone out with tons of guys I work with. How else are you supposed to meet people?"

"But . . ."

"But what?" Cheryl was in attack mode. I didn't know why she was so worked up about this A. J. thing, but it was making me a little uncomfortable.

"But you're you!" I blurted. "You know how to talk to people. You know how to flirt!"

"Don't be silly," Cheryl said. "I've seen you flirt before, Miss Heaven Kogo. You can do anything you want if you put your mind to it."

I sipped my Cherry Coke thoughtfully. "Honestly? I think I'm still too wrapped up in the Hiro thing." As soon as the words were out of my mouth, something clicked open in my brain. I realized how true those words actually were—and how nice it felt to admit my feelings to somebody.

"Now, *that's* a good reason," Cheryl said. "But you have to get over it. It's just not going anywhere."

"I know, I know." The tension between us had dissolved, and she was back to her old fun-loving self. I decided I might as well bring up the Marcus issue while things were good. Just in a casual way.

"So what about Marcus?" I asked. "How's that going?"

"Awesome," Cheryl said. "But no big thing. We're just having fun. And there's *a lot* of fun to be had." She winked.

"Has he asked you to any parties yet?"

"Not yet. But he told me he has a bunch of events coming up next month, and he's going to give me VIP passes for all of them. It's going to be fabulous."

The more Cheryl talked, the less inclined I was to burst her bubble. But if I didn't, I'd be doing exactly what Hiro had done to me. Keeping it to myself was *not* an option.

"So Cheryl—there's something I have to tell you," I mumbled, sipping my soda. Might as well get it out of the way.

"Uh-oh. Sounds serious." Cheryl drew the corners of her mouth down in mock severity.

"It kind of is. . . ." I struggled for the right words. Friendship wasn't exactly something I'd had a lot of experience with, and I didn't want Cheryl to be angry.

"Spit it out," Cheryl said, ever the practical one. "I promise I won't be mad."

"Okay. It's just that . . . A. J. told me tonight that Marcus is a gangbanger. I thought you should know."

For a moment Cheryl just stared at me. Then she threw

back her head and let out her signature deep, throaty laugh.

"Heaven, you are too much!" Cheryl said, recovering herself. "You can be such a baby sometimes! I mean, it's like you were raised on an island!"

"I was." I didn't see the joke.

"You know what I mean." Cheryl laughed again and shook her head. I tried not to be irritated, but it was clear she was laughing *at* me, not *with* me. I didn't see anything funny about it at all. "But really," Cheryl continued, "thanks for telling me and all, but I already knew."

"What?" Just then our pancakes arrived, and we both kept our mouths shut until the waitress refilled Cheryl's coffee cup and left us alone.

"So what?" Cheryl answered, hacking at her pancakes. "What's the big deal?"

"The big deal?" I asked, shocked. "He's a gang member. Doesn't that bother you a little bit? I mean, it's probably not the safest thing to be hanging out with him, you know."

"Don't be silly, Heaven. You're really making a huge deal out of nothing. I mean, half of L.A. under twenty-five probably thinks they're a gangbanger these days just because they have a posse of friends. You're unfamiliar with this territory is all."

"Just because I'm not the most experienced person in the world doesn't mean I have no morals," I snapped. "Stop being so condescending."

"Oh, so now it's a moral thing?" Cheryl asked, her smile fading.

"I'm not saying that—"

"That's what you said," Cheryl interrupted, fixing me with a steely gaze. She could be really fierce when she wanted to be.

"Okay, that's what I said," I admitted. "Yes. Yes, I think it's a moral issue. I mean, who knows what his business is, how he makes his money? What if he sells drugs? Why would you want to be involved with that?"

"He doesn't sell drugs," Cheryl said coldly.

"Do you know that for sure?" I asked, pushing my pancakes away. Whatever appetite I'd had was gone. "Believe me, I've had some experience with the kind of people who get involved with organized crime. And it's not like in the movies. People get hurt. People die."

"What experience? What are you talking about?" Cheryl looked unconvinced. "You're starting to sound like one of those weird commercials—you know, like, if you fill up your car with gas or you go to a party where someone's smoking a cigarette, you're helping out terrorists."

"That's not what I'm saying at all. You're twisting my words. I just want you to be safe. That's the bottom line."

"I think this conversation is over," Cheryl said, looking away as she threw down her fork. The people at the table next to us looked over, and I blushed.

"Cheryl, please listen," I whispered. "That's not all—

there's something about him. . . ." I took a deep breath. "I think he was hitting on me the other night." As soon as the words left my mouth, I regretted having said them. Even though I knew it was true, I could tell that Cheryl wasn't in a believing mood.

"You are so full of it." Cheryl shook her head. "Why are you trying to sabotage me?"

"I'm absolutely not. I just don't want to keep any secrets from you."

"Well, it's a little late for that, isn't it?" Cheryl's eyes blazed. "Why so trusting all of a sudden?"

I started to panic. This was not going like I'd planned. "This is different," I pleaded.

"You're right. It's different because you're acting like a jealous baby. You totally don't understand the kind of guy Marcus is. He was probably just being sweet to you because you're my roommate. And you overreacted, as usual. You know, men are not the enemy, Heaven."

"I know," I said. I didn't want to argue anymore.

"So why don't you just mind your own business from now on?" Cheryl snapped.

"Excuse me for a second," I said quietly, and headed for the bathroom. Once inside, I slipped into one of the cherry red stalls. My stomach hurt from nerves. I stared at the silhouette of a roller-skating girl on the inside of the stall door and tried to think what to do next. Should I apologize? For what? Caring enough to not want Cheryl to get hurt? I wondered if Cheryl would ask me to leave the apartment. Then what would I do?

Everything seemed suddenly overwhelming. If Cheryl didn't want to be my friend anymore, then who would I have left? I imagined myself moving into some seedy motel until I saved enough for my own place, shuttling back and forth between Vibe and a dangerous, depressing motel room. No one would know who I was, and no one would care what I did. I'd be completely, finally, totally alone, just another nameless, faceless girl walking the streets of L.A. And if whoever it was that was after me finally succeeded in getting to me, then it would be sayonara, Heaven. Poof. I'd disappear just like Teddy had.

I wrapped my arms around myself, feeling chilled. My watch said 5:00 A.M. Thank goodness I had the next day off. I took a deep breath and decided to apologize. Better to smooth things over. I'd done all I could, and it was clear I couldn't risk this last, delicate friendship over something as silly as a bad news boyfriend. Cheryl was a big girl. If she wanted to be with Marcus, then who was I to tell her not to?

When I got back to the table, Cheryl was staring into her compact and applying lip gloss. She ignored me when I sat down.

"I'm sorry," I said lamely. "I shouldn't have overreacted that way. You're right. It's none of my business." Cheryl kept applying her gloss, still not looking at me. "I just thought you should know," I added.

"Well, thanks for nothing," Cheryl said in a steely voice,

snapping the little mirror shut. "Next time keep it to your-self." She picked up the check and dug through her bag, looking for money.

"Let me get it," I said, picking up the check. Cheryl looked up at me for a second, then shrugged.

"Well, *that's* a change," she said sarcastically.

I felt tears coming to my eyes again. It wasn't like Cheryl to be so cruel. She knew I couldn't help it when I was broke. Or maybe she didn't know—after all, there was so much I hadn't told her, and maybe she really did think that I'd quit Life Bytes just out of laziness or boredom.

"Cheryl," I said quietly, "I know I owe you rent, but I have that money now. I can give it to you when we get home."

"Whatever," Cheryl said, and strode out of the restau-rant. I paid the check and followed her outside. Before com-ing to L.A., I'd never thought about money once in my whole life. The money was always there. Sure, there were things my father wouldn't let me buy, but that had nothing to do with the cost—it was all about what he found "appropri-ate." I'd never thought about what it took to stay afloat out in the real world. And now that I knew the Kogo money wasn't clean, I felt even guiltier about the lavish life I had lived—and the fact that it hadn't prepared me to support myself. I vowed I would never take a loan from anyone again, no matter what happened. I would make my own way if it killed me.

Neither of us said a word on the cab ride home, and

Cheryl went into her bedroom and slammed the door as soon as we were in the house.

I felt empty inside. I pushed away a vision of the dirty motel room I'd imagined earlier.

I'd figure it all out tomorrow. There had to be some way to make it right.

When I told my boys about the job, they were like, "What's up with that, G.?" I'll admit, it's not the kind of thing I usually get into, but it seemed like an easy gig. And the money? Nothing like the going rates around here, all these cheap washed-up celebrities and folks "in the business." Uh-uh. They were offering a lot of Benjamins up front. Cold, hard cash. When I told the boys what they'd each be getting for doing their part, they shut up fast—they know what side their bread is buttered on. Only thing they said was, "Why you always get the fun part, G.?" I just laughed. When you're the leader, you're the leader. There are perks.

Now, Cheryl, she's a nice little perk. It was almost too easy getting her attention. When I first saw her, I thought she might put up a fight—she's that type of girl, you know the one, with a tight little body and that punky look going on. Looks like she might be all feminist and whatnot. But she turned out to be just like all the rest of them . . . can't say no to the Marcus-grade smile, uh-uh. By the end of that first night she was begging for more of me. The second time I saw her, she was wrapped around my finger.

Heaven, now that's a different story. My charms don't seem to have impressed the little princess. The little lost princess. But it makes no difference. She likes her friend, and her friend likes me, and that's all that has to happen. When I first saw her, I thought for a second that I might have been better off putting the moves on her—now that's a girl who's got it going on. I like them tall and hard like that. She could be a model if she wanted to, no joke. But no—too much trouble. I made exactly the right move. Get the friend. Like candy from a baby. No mess.

Poor Cheryl. But that's the way the ball rolls. If Heaven's the kind of girl I think she is, she'll do what she needs to do. We'll take care of Heaven, and that will be the end of it.

Everybody's happy. Except maybe the little lost princess. But that's not my problem.

Business is business.

MARCUS

8

I woke up at ten feeling like I hadn't slept at all. My aching muscles and restless mind kept me from falling back asleep. Pulling the covers over my head, I tried to talk myself out of the funk. I could apologize to Cheryl again. Go for a run to loosen up my sore muscles. Call Hiro on the phone and make things right, even if I wasn't yet ready to commit to training with him again. But where would that get me?

I threw off my comforter and wandered out into the living room. Cheryl's door was ajar—I peeked into her room, which looked, as always, as though it had been hit by a tornado, and saw that her bed was empty. She must have had to work early again today, which was probably for the best, as she no doubt still hated my guts. I wondered where she got the energy to party all night and work all day. Some people were lucky that way. Unfortunately, I wasn't one of them.

I flopped onto the couch and flipped on the TV, much like I had in the weeks after I quit Life Bytes, when I was recovering from the Karen kidnapping nightmare. It was late morning, and *The View* was on, which I hated. What was more boring than watching Barbara Walters preside over a bunch of stupid, boring conversational topics? I reached lazily for the remote but came up empty-handed. It was sitting on top of the TV. Too unmotivated to get it, I watched the girls talk about "men who say no but mean yes" and learned the interesting fact that sometimes, men who say no actually mean yes. Fascinating stuff. Disgusted, I hurled a cushion at the TV in an attempt to hit the power button off. The TV cut off with a squawk.

Pathetic. I was pathetic. I had the day off, and I couldn't think of anything constructive to do. This was my life, and it was ticking by uselessly. I looked at the phone, and it reminded me about my decision not to call Mieko. I felt so lonely, I almost changed my mind, but it would be the middle of the night in Tokyo—and I knew that wasn't the right thing to do, anyway.

I sighed, staring at the ceiling. Now I had a job, and I could pay my rent, but without training, my life here in L.A. really was pointless. I was a shot girl, with no prospects, no college education, and no family. And now it seemed like I would never be able to figure out who was trying to harm me. That is, until they finally caught up with me. Then I'd know everything, but it would be too late. I'd be well on my way to dead.

I thought about Konishi. Mieko had told Hiro that his condition was still the same. No better. But he had said my name. I wondered for a second if seeing me might help him to recover, then discarded the thought. Everyone around me seemed to get hurt, and the best thing I could do for my father was to let him get well in peace—and safety. I buried my face in the sofa and tried to clear my head.

Corn Pops? Maybe food would help. I fixed myself a heaping bowl and brought it back to the couch, tripping on my messenger bag along the way. As I wiped up the milk that had sloshed onto the floor, I suddenly remembered the Funkitout CD that A. J. had given me. I slipped it into the CD player and munched on my cereal.

The song, like most raps, started with a thumping bass line. After a few measures a higher melodic beat started up and surged over the bass. I nodded in time to the music. It was a catchy tune, all right, with a great sample. After a few grunts and groans the lyrics kicked in:

> *I wanna check you out*
> *Check you out, hey yo yo*
> *I'm packin' cash like Konishi Kogo*

I stopped in midchew. *Please tell me I'm still asleep and this is just some crazy nightmare,* I thought.

> *Got my girls in a huddle on the club couch*

I jumped up and jammed the back button on the CD player, starting the song over. Had I really heard what I thought I heard?

Yes. And this was no nightmare. The song went on:

> *When I go out I don't need to say much*
> *All the boys they ask, "Where's Heaven at?"*
> *If I knew I'd have to kill you with my gat*
> *Nobody knows where baby has gone*
> *Sing hey, hey . . .*

Oh. No. I sat frozen as the song continued, multiple voices chanting the *heys* and *hos* of the chorus. How many people had heard this song? How many understood the lyrics?

> *She was a red, a red-hot ma-ma,*
> *Society girl in her silk pa-ja-mas,*
> *Disappeared in a cloud on her weddin' night,*
> *Kogo style, maybe Daddy was right,*
> *Nobody knows where Heaven has gone*
> *Sing hey, hey . . .*

After three more similar verses the song ended. I listened to it one more time. The song was obviously about me. *Think, Heaven, think,* I told myself. What did it mean? I resisted the urge to pick up the phone and call Hiro. First I had to figure out what the hell was going on. Who was Funkitout? How much airplay was the single getting? I picked up the CD case—DJ Slavo had printed out the picture of the band from the original cover—four nondescript Japanese guys in baggy pants and sunglasses. There was no information about them at all.

I rubbed my eyes, trying to think clearly through my fatigue and nervousness. I knew there had been articles in the Japanese papers about my disappearance. That wasn't unusual. My father was one of the most famous men in Japan, and the tabloids had regularly tried to get dirt on Ohiko and me, heirs to the "Kogo Empire." When my engagement to Teddy Yukemura was announced, the seedy journalists had tried just about every trick in the book to get information about the wedding—as far as I'd been able to tell at the time, that was one of the reasons the ceremony had been moved to L.A. In the States we were just a bunch of rich Japanese—not the national celebrities we were back home. Soon after the wedding, though, someone had leaked my photo to the American press, and they'd run it on the news—"Heiress Missing After Bizarre Incident at Beverly Wilshire" or something like that.

As far as I knew, nothing had been run about me recently. But my father was still in a coma, and I had a hard time imagining that subservient Mieko would be able to do the kind of damage control for which Konishi was famous. Not to mention the fact that with the new job at Vibe and everything else distracting me, I hadn't been checking the papers the way I had before.

I ran to my room and pulled on a pair of jeans and a T-shirt. Book Soup, a bookstore and newsstand in West Hollywood, carried all the international and domestic papers. I could search through them, then go meet Hiro and tell him about the song and anything else I might find. I threw the CD in my messenger bag and headed out.

The bus lumbered down Sunset Boulevard, and I stared out the window into the bright California sun. The people on the street seemed so carefree and happy. I nearly ran the block from the bus stop to the store. People stared at me as I rushed over to the periodicals and began pulling papers like the *Asahi Shinbun* off the racks and pawing through them.

Half an hour later I breathed a sigh of relief. I'd come up empty-handed. Still feeling giddy, I decided to bus it back to the Virgin megastore farther east on Sunset. If the single was there, I might have a problem. As the bus passed the famous Chateau Marmont Hotel, where the stars had stayed for almost as long as there had been stars, I thought about how weird L.A. was—it was almost like three cities in one—the city of the celebrities, sheltered and unreal, filled with glittering parties and beautiful people; the city of everybody else, waiters and waitresses trying to make it, people and families going to work and school every day like the rest of America—and then there was the city I lived in. A city of whispers and dark places, a city the light of the sun couldn't reach.

At Virgin my luck changed. The single was there, lodged among the other imports and independent label offerings. I bought the original copy and took it outside, where I sat on a bench and unwrapped it. No more clues to be had. The original insert just gave the band members' names, none of which I recognized, and offered a few more pictures and the address of their recording studio, in Tokyo. I studied the photos of the band members for the telltale tattoos that symbolized membership in the yakuza. Nothing.

Sitting on the bench, I though about how Ohiko and I would have laughed if something like this had happened back in the day, when we still lived at home and when it still seemed like we might eventually lead some kind of normal life. We would have got such a kick out of it to have a hip-hop song about our family. The songs about me from back when I survived the plane crash were in a different vein—just stupid little tributes people recorded in their basements or home studios that the radio played for a few months when the country was gripped by "Heaven Fever." My nanny, Harumi, had recorded them all and played them for me when I was older. I wondered how many people the Funkitout single would reach. If A. J. and DJ Slavo knew it, it had to be getting pretty wide play even outside of Japan.

How long would it take before someone made the connection?

One thing I knew for sure—I'd definitely be *mis*-translating those lyrics for A. J.

I stood up and headed back to the bus stop. A small part of me relished the thought of giving Hiro the bad news. Dumping me wouldn't be quite as easy as he'd hoped.

When I was a child, my nanny, Okuma-san, used to tell me the story of Urashima, the kind fisher lad who rescued a sea tortoise from a group of mischievous young boys who were about to torture it to death. After Urashima convinced the boys to give him the tortoise, he released it into the sea, but the tortoise returned the next day and offered to take Urashima to the underwater palace of the Dragon King of the Sea. Riding on the tortoise's back, Urashima visited the kingdom and there met the Sea King's daughter, a beautiful princess. The princess told him that he saved her, for she had chosen the form of the tortoise to explore the world outside the kingdom's walls.

In my favorite part of the story Urashima married the princess and she showed him all the delights of the kingdom. But Urashima, after the first delight had passed, realized that his parents would be devastated by his absence. Sadly, the princess conceded that he must return to land. But before he left, she gave him a black lacquered box tied with a red string. "This is Tamate-Bako," she told him, "the 'Box of the Jewel Hand.' You must accept this gift from me, but you can never open it."

Urashima agreed and, with a heavy heart, returned to land. But something was different. Although the landscape remained unchanged, the faces that passed him on the streets of his village were strange to him. Urashima then learned from a passerby that three hundred years had passed in what seemed but a few weeks under the sea. His parents were dead. There was nothing left for him on land, in his village. Unable to figure out what else to do, Urashima presumed that the only way for him to return to his beloved princess was to disobey her and open Tamate-Bako. He untied the red string and opened the box, and a red mist floated out. Within moments his skin wrinkled, his body shrank, his hair turned white, and he was transformed into an ancient man.

"Now, listen, Konishi-chan," Okuma-san would say as she finished the sad tale, "that is what happens to young boys who misbehave. You must always do as you are told."

When I first was injured, this story came back to me, and it was as though I were Urashima. I could feel myself sinking under the waves, the world outside still there but far above me, untouchable. I can hear the voices through my watery shroud: Mieko's voice, her murmur, and the things she whispers in my ear.

I must get back to the surface. They are holding me captive here in this sea world, keeping me away, and my greatest fear is that too much time will have passed before I return, if I ever do. I must help Heaven, warn her of the forces that are working against her.

I must leave this floating blue-green world, for in this incarnation, it is not I who holds the Tamate-Bako, but Heaven.

Opening it will kill her.

I must return.

Konishi

9

My hands were sweating when I got to the dojo. I'd learned my lesson from last time and had stopped to call Hiro's house from a pay phone. There was no answer. But it wasn't until I was pushing open the smooth wooden door of the dojo that I considered that Hiro might not even be there. I'd been so shocked by the song and my mad investigative rush into West Hollywood that it hadn't even occurred to me Hiro could just as easily be at work.

"Heaven? Oh my God! Hi!" Sami, a tall blond instructor at the dojo, looked up from her seat at the front desk. "I haven't seen *you* in a while!"

"Hi, Sami," I said, smiling. She was one of my favorite people at the dojo and one of the only instructors (beside Hiro and Karen, obviously) who always took the time to ask how I was doing.

"Where have you been?" Sami asked. "Do you want some tea or something?"

"No, thanks. I was in last week, actually—I didn't see you, though."

"Yeah, I was on vacation. I went to Vegas!"

"Wow, that sounds awesome!" I said. Sami's smile was infectious. "Did you like it?" Not for the first time I wondered if I should pack my bags and head for Vegas myself. I could find my tutor, Katie, and we could start a new life there together. The only problem was that I'd left her mother's phone number in the hotel (along with everything else I owned) the night of the wedding, and information had no listing for her.

"It was great," Sami said, "but pretty intense. I don't think I could take it for more than a few days. I liked the slots a little too much, if you know what I mean!"

"How did you get there?" I asked—I didn't really know what she meant.

"I flew—they have ultracheap tickets, and you're there in an hour. I think I paid about ninety dollars round trip."

"That's crazy," I said. "So cheap. Do you need a passport to get on the plane?" My passport was something else I had left behind.

"Passport?" Sami asked, giving me a weird look. "No. All you need is an ID. Haven't you ever flown anywhere in the States?"

"Nope," I said, trying to sound casual. "Just international."

No flight to Vegas for me—somehow I doubted my fake ID would pass muster at the airport, especially with all the increased security these days. If I decided to get out of L.A., I'd have to take a bus or something.

"Hey," I said, "is Hiro around?"

"Heaven? What a surprise." Karen walked over to the front desk, looking distinctly *un*-surprised. She was wearing street clothes and looked like she was on her way out of the dojo. "I suppose you're looking for Hiro?"

I looked over at Sami, whose smile had disappeared. She seemed clued in to the tension between Karen and me.

"I've got to run this paperwork upstairs. Good to see you, Heaven." Sami slipped out from behind the desk and made her escape.

"Bye, Sam," I said, desperately wishing she had stayed.

"Well?" Karen asked.

"Actually, yeah," I said. Talk about dispensing with the small talk. The only person who'd ever looked less happy to see me was my adoptive mother, Mieko. In fact, the only time I'd seen Karen look so tired and out of it was after the kidnapping. Today she had dark circles under her eyes, and her normally smooth hair was held back in a messy ponytail. Not that she didn't look hot—now she just looked gorgeous *and* needy.

"Too bad. He's at work." Karen crossed her arms and leaned back on the desk. "Nothing I can help with?"

I shook my head. "Sorry. I have some information I need to let him know about."

Karen looked at me for a second as though she was trying to think of what to say, then she unfolded her arms and
stood up straighter.

"Come with me for a second," she said, walking toward
one of the practice rooms. On the way down the hallway I
said hello to a few other people I recognized from when I'd
been at the dojo all day every day. Every single one of them
looked at me strangely. Like I was a ghost.

"Why don't you tell me what you need to talk to Hiro
about?" Karen said, her voice cold as she shut the door to
the practice room. "I'll give him the message."

"I'd really rather not," I said, nervous, but irritated at
her for trying to boss me around. "You know Hiro thinks
it's in your best interests not to know about what's
going on with me. And you've already had to deal with
the consequences."

"Exactly. Your shenanigans got me kidnapped. So I'm
not too worried that one more piece of information will land
me in a situation much worse than that."

Shenanigans? What did she think this was? A game of
cops and robbers?

"Karen, you don't understand—"

"Oh, I understand perfectly," Karen said, her voice
barely controlled. Her mouth twitched as she crossed her
arms again. She was buff, that was for sure. "I understand
that ever since you and Hiro had your little *conversation*
the other day, he's been a total and complete wreck. He's

preoccupied, distracted—he's been doing nothing but working and meditating."

Karen's information was surprising. Somehow I'd imagined that after Hiro got the Mieko call off his chest that day, he and Karen had just skipped happily back into their lovey-dovey, newly Heaven-free lifestyle without another thought. It was news to me that he was as upset by our fight as I'd been. I couldn't help being a little happy about it.

"Are you *smiling?*" Karen asked fiercely.

Oops. I straightened my face. I really hadn't meant to. "No," I said seriously. "I'm just nervous and trying to think of something to say."

"Why don't you say, 'Okay, Karen, I'll leave your boyfriend alone'?"

"I can't," I said, growing angry.

"Why not? Hiro's life was normal before you came into it. And I don't know who you are or why you're here, but I want you gone."

"You don't know anything about me," I snapped, "so you're in no position to tell me what to do. Besides, I think you're forgetting that if it wasn't for me and if it wasn't for Hiro *helping* me, you'd still be tied up in a dark room some-where. Or worse—"

"Give me a break," Karen yelled, interrupting me. "If it hadn't been for you, I wouldn't have been kidnapped in the first place. I was planning on staying at Hiro's that night, but you had to come along with your 'little girl lost' act, needing to talk, and that's why I went home at that hour."

She'd really gone over the top. It was like a totally different Karen was standing before me than the one I knew. Sure, I'd suspected before that having to share Hiro with me and my problems was less than optimal, but this—all of a sudden she was like Alicia Silverstone in *The Crush* or something. An Asian Alicia Silverstone. But still. If her protectiveness of Hiro wasn't so awful and desperate, it would have been funny. I certainly didn't see myself as quite the home wrecker she did.

"Yes, I came by that night," I said, still picturing Karen standing ominously by the side of a glowing blue pool, "but no one told you to leave. All I needed was five minutes of Hiro's time, but you wanted to be independent and go home by yourself when no one even cared—you could have gone into the other room for a couple of minutes, or—"

"But I didn't!" Karen yelled, cutting me off again. "I left. And I got kidnapped. By people who were after *you!* Do you know what things are like for me now? Do you know how it feels to have to watch your back every time you leave your house? To hold your breath every time you unlock your car door, hoping that no one's right behind you?"

"Welcome to my world!" I shouted. "Welcome to my freaking world!" I took a step toward her, and Karen finally shut up, looking a little taken aback. Well, she wasn't the only one who could let loose. And I was just getting started. "Who the hell do you think you are? Look—I'm really sorry you got kidnapped, but I live with that feeling *every day*. They didn't mean to take you. They meant to take me. They wanted to *kill me*. And they've already come after me again since then." Karen's face had hardened—I didn't think I was getting through to her, but I didn't want to stop. It felt too good to vent.

"As soon as I finish one fight, another one starts. Do you think that's fun? Huh? They killed my brother right in front of me. And my father's in a coma. If the attack had gone a little differently, I would have had to watch his murder, too. And I'm sorry if my needing Hiro's help means you don't get to have your perfect life right now, but I can't do anything about it!"

My voice shook as I uttered my last words. Karen still looked unmoved, aloof. It was clear she hated me and would do anything to get me out of Hiro's life. The truth, however much of it she knew or understood, made no difference to her. And I didn't really care what she knew anymore. That was her problem. I'd always known she was a perfectionist, but I hadn't banked on her being willing to fight so hard in order to put the Hiro part of her life into apple-pie order.

"Too bad," Karen said evenly. "But it doesn't change anything. You better stay away from Hiro. You've already quit your training twice. So the way I see it, you've run out of passes. Go find someone else to help you." Karen walked toward me, and I almost laughed as I realized she was getting ready to spar with me. The last thing I needed was to get into a physical confrontation with her. Hiro would never forgive me.

"Why don't you just calm down?" I asked her nervously.

"Why don't you get the hell out of here? And get the hell out of my life while you're at it," Karen hissed, putting her face close to mine. I stepped back, and Karen followed.

"You're not his mother," I said, instinctively raising my arms in case she lost control of her temper. "You don't speak for him." Suddenly the ridiculousness of the whole discussion hit me. Here we were arguing about Hiro as if he was a twelve-year-old boy! As if *we* were twelve-year-old girls! And although I didn't have much experience (okay, any) in this kind of thing, it seemed pretty absurd. Like Catwoman and Batgirl duking it out over Batman—or was it Robin they were fighting about? I couldn't remember, but for a second I imagined Karen clad in black leather from head to toe—it was kind of a scary image.

"No," Karen said. "I speak for myself. So I'm going to say it one more time. *Lay off.* Figure it out yourself. Get yourself a boyfriend of your own to help you."

That's when it hit me. Karen was *jealous.* It was so obvious. But I'd spent so much time feeling inferior to Karen, who was so self-composed, so *together,* that I'd never thought she might view me as competition for Hiro's affection. For his time, maybe, but not his heart.

Could she see something that I couldn't? My heart bounced in my chest. Was there any possibility . . .

"Did you hear me?" Karen barked, and I jerked my head back. I wasn't even mad anymore. Her desperation seemed truly, completely pathetic.

"I heard you," I said quietly. There was nothing to be done. If Hiro wanted to see me, he would come and see me. Until then I could spend a lot of time hoping that maybe Hiro would eventually see this side of Karen and maybe think twice about wanting to be with her.

"And?" Karen pressed, still in the moment.

"Good-bye, Karen," I said calmly, which only seemed to infuriate her more. She stayed right up in my face, her body taut, her stance defensive. But all the fight had gone out of me. I'd never admit it to *her,* but she'd more than achieved her purpose. No, I wouldn't tell Hiro about the song. I wouldn't ask for his help or advice. Not because of Karen, but because of him. I didn't want to mess up his life anymore. I didn't want to drag him down with me.

"That's it? That's all you have to say?" Karen shouted as I opened the practice room door.

"Get over it," I whispered under my breath, just to make myself feel better, then slammed the door behind me. I ran out of the dojo.

I was trembling a little when I got outside. No matter how off base Karen had been, it wasn't any fun getting yelled at—or threatened, for that matter. When I went over the whole scene in my head, I thought of a hundred ways I could have handled it better—snappy comebacks I could have made, biting, witty responses that would have left Karen apologetic and in tears. But it was too late now, and mostly I just wished I hadn't set foot in the dojo at all. Now I had yet another unpleasant encounter to mull over, along with all the others. It felt like I had the plague. Was there anyone left who didn't hate me? I thought of Teddy and wished all over again it had been him at Vibe that night. Then at least I'd have *one* person around who liked me, even if I wasn't quite sure how I felt about him.

I missed Ohiko. I missed my father.

By the time I got home, the late afternoon sunlight was casting long shadows over the front yards and gardens of Dawson Street. The house was exactly as I had left it—the half-eaten bowl of Corn Pops on the coffee table, the cushion lying at the base of the TV where I had hurled it—and still no Cheryl. I turned on some lights and began to clean up.

I needed to forget. And the only place I could think of to do it was Vibe. But first I'd need a nap.

Dancing was hard work, too—but least it was the kind of work I couldn't screw up.

Things aren't how they used to be with Karen. Since the kidnapping she's become more needy—not exactly the strong, independent woman I became close to, the woman who was so composed and patient—my lotus flower. Part of that is normal, I know—it's just the healing process at work. She has anger and fear that must be channeled into a new strength. That takes time.

What worries me is not her dependence, exactly, but the bitterness she seems to feel toward Heaven. And her sudden inability to accept the choices I make in my life. When Karen came over after Heaven and I fought the last time, I told her that I needed to be by myself to meditate, and for the first time she didn't understand. She cried. Begged me not to see Heaven again. "It's tearing you apart," she said, "and I need you right now."

I knew when I became involved with Karen that the relationship might distract me from my path—at the time I did not care. Karen seemed like a stable presence, a blessing in a life that Heaven's arrival turned upside down. She was a link to the present, to the life that I'd built here in Los Angeles. And I needed that link when Heaven, who seemed a reminder of my past, came to claim my attention. I needed Karen when Heaven's predicament threatened to topple my carefully constructed new life. But the bushido says that a samurai must be single-minded in the pursuit of his duty. Romantic relationships fulfill only the needs of the body—and the fleeting desires of the present. And

perhaps I have been unwise in thinking that Karen could save me.

Perhaps being with her has only been an escape.

As I meditate, it occurs to me that no matter what I do now, I will hurt her. And this gives me great pain. What is worse, when I picture a life without Karen in it, I have to admit to myself that I do not picture myself alone.

It is not the solitude of the samurai my heart yearns for.

It is another path, with another woman.

Hiro

10

Thump, thump, thump . . . the bass laid down a smooth, consistent line—a shining path for my body to follow when the melody or the wild vocals veered off track—my very own trail of bread crumbs through the song. *Now* this *is music,* I thought. The crowd of dancers pressed tightly around me, and in the warm grip of the groove it didn't matter that I was alone. I was part of something larger and more pure than anything I could imagine.

The song ended, and when the DJ put on a slower groove, I tied my sweaty hair up into a bun and walked to the bar. Being in the zone on the dance floor reminded me of the mission Hiro had given me before our "breakup." Although I'd had plenty of time to meditate—what with Cheryl giving me the silent treatment—I just hadn't been able to get up the energy to do it, and I had *way* too much to think about to "clear my head." Training seemed so far away . . . and was I even *supposed* to continue with my mission now that I'd lost my trainer? I pressed my worries away. Tonight was for fun—and dancing would just have to be my Zen koan for now.

"Having a good time, Miss Heaven?" A. J. called out to me as I squeezed between a couple of girls who were trying to get his attention. I ignored their dirty looks. I was going to forget about my problems *and* everyone else's.

"Great!" I yelled, laughing. "But I'm thirsty."

"One vodka cranberry, coming right up!" A. J. tossed the bottle of vodka in the air behind his back, took a step, and caught it.

"Gotta keep in practice, you know?" A. J. said, setting the drink in front of me. "And what can I do for you ladies?" he asked the girls next to me with a little bow. I picked up my drink and turned around to watch the action on the dance floor. Vibe was packed tonight, and part of me wished that I was working so I could make even more money. But I also needed a break—and I could tell the dancing was doing me good. My body was used to a lot of physical activity, and since I'd stopped training, I'd started to feel sort of sluggish. I reminded myself again that tonight was for doing, not thinking. And one of the things I was doing was working on my dance moves.

"So, Heaven, what'd you think about the Funkitout song?" A. J. leaned toward me as he pulled a couple of bottles of beer out from the cooler under the bar. I choked a little on my drink. I'd been hoping he'd forget about the CD.

"I loved it!" I said, overcompensating.

"Wow. Really? Hold on—" A. J. delivered the beers, then came back over. "It's pretty catchy, huh?"

"Mmm . . . definitely." I nodded vaguely. "And I love how the crowd voices kind of come in on the refrain—it's not very original, but it's a good hook."

"So what's the song about? Slavo's been after me to ask you. Be right back." A customer at the other end of the bar was waving a twenty in the air. I chewed on a piece of ice—this shouldn't be that hard. All A. J. knew was that the song was about a girl named Heaven, so . . .

"Here." A. J. appeared with another vodka cranberry.

"You trying to get me drunk?" I joked.

"Why not? It's your night off."

"Good point." I exchanged my empty glass for the full one and set to work on Vodka Cranberry: The Sequel.

"So? The song?"

"Oh. Yeah. Well, it's about this girl named Heaven who falls in love with this boy. Nothing that exciting. She does him wrong, then he breaks up with her, and she comes back to him when he proves to her that he's better than all the other guys. Just the standard stuff."

"But don't you think it's weird that it would be about a girl named Heaven? I mean, that's a pretty uncommon name."

"Actually, in Japan it isn't," I lied, apologizing to A. J. in my head. Some goodwill ambassador I was. Disseminating false information about my native country.

"Really? I didn't know that."

"Yep." I nodded, warming up. "In fact, it's a name that brings good luck, some say. So when you take that, combined with the subject matter of the lyrics, it's kind of a perfect fit. There are a bunch of folk songs written about a girl named Heaven, even. We used to sing them in school." I didn't know if it was the drink or what, but suddenly I was lying like a champ. Without even a blush. Normally when I tried to evade the truth I turned into a bumbling idiot.

"Interesting . . . ," A. J. said, "It's funny that even someplace like Japan, hip-hop incorporates older genres—same as here."

"*Excuse me!*" shouted a girl wearing a dashiki at the end of the bar. A. J. rolled his eyes.

"Duty calls." He poured vodka into a shot glass. "On the house, of course," he said before moving off. *What the hell,* I thought, and drank it down.

I stood at the bar for a while watching A. J. pouring drinks. He was so quick on his feet—*He'd be good at karate,* I thought. Nice hand-eye coordination. It occurred to me that A. J. was pretty cute, really, and definitely easy to talk to. Why *couldn't* I have a crush on someone like that? Maybe Cheryl was right—aside from him being my boss, he'd be a perfect boyfriend. I allowed myself to picture a world in which A. J. and I went on dates just like every other couple in L.A. We could go have dinner and walk the Santa Monica pier, take a ride on the roller coaster, hold hands. We could go for day trips to Big Sur and hike along the coast—do all the happy, carefree things I'd read about in guidebooks before coming to L.A. Things my life right now wouldn't allow.

"Well, if it isn't Heaven—Johnson, is it?" A hand slid around my waist. Marcus. I instinctively jerked back, but Marcus's hand stayed firmly planted on my hip, his arm clasping me too close for comfort.

"Is Cheryl here?" I asked, trying to subtly wriggle out of his grip. It was the first question that popped into my head.

"Funny. I was about to ask you the same thing." Up close, I could see that Marcus had a thin scar running from the outer corner of his left eye all the way down to his jawbone. I couldn't help staring at it.

"All the ladies wanna know where I got this from," Marcus said in his deadly, deep voice. "Do you?"

"Not really," I said, blushing and pushing his arm off me. He frightened me. I wanted to be back on the dance floor, back where Marcus didn't exist.

"Aw, come on. You know you do." Marcus traced the scar with his index finger as he moved closer. I saw A. J. shoot us a look, and I prayed that he would come and rescue me.

"Well?" I looked him in the eye. Might as well get it over with.

"You see? Everyone wants to know." Marcus took a sip of his drink. "When I was twelve, I was playing out in the street with some of my neighborhood homies. Stickball or some shit like that. And this one kid, his name was Vincent, he started giving me lots of mouth, you know? Like, 'Marcus, you gotta pitch that ball harder,' and, 'Marcus, why you messin' up our team with your sorry-ass playin'? So when it was my turn to bat and when Vincent started in again . . ." Marcus stirred his drink with his finger and licked it slowly. I had a feeling I didn't want to hear the rest of the story.

". . . I beat the crap out of him." Marcus looked pleased with himself. Suddenly I felt like I was going to throw up. I couldn't believe Cheryl had actually made out (and whatever else) with this loser. She was worth twelve of him.

"That doesn't really explain how you got the scar," I said, trying to keep my voice sounding strong and unintimidated.

"Oh—that was from when they pulled me off him. I tripped and hit a rusty old car fender. It could have been much worse." Marcus fingered the scar. *Could he be any grosser?* I wondered.

"Marcus, whatsup." A. J. came over, saving me from having to comment on Marcus's grotesque little reminiscence. They shook hands.

"Not much, dog. Why don't you get Heaven and me a drink?" A. J. looked at me, and I nodded. I needed something to stop the anxiety that was washing through me in waves.

"So, that brings us back to your little friend Cheryl," Marcus said. "Is she going to be here tonight?"

"I don't know," I said honestly. "I haven't seen her since last night."

"Oh, no?" Marcus said, raising his eyebrows. "And why is that?"

I shrugged. A. J. appeared with our drinks and ran off again. He was too busy to rescue me completely.

"Wanna dance?" Marcus asked, his hot breath filling my ear.

"Um . . . no, thanks," I said.

"Why not?" Marcus whispered. "I've seen your moves, and they're pretty fly."

"Why, if it isn't my old friend Marcus!" Nina leaned across the bar and planted a kiss on Marcus's lips, which he returned. What a jerk.

"Hello, sweetheart. How's the night treating you?" Marcus loosened his hold on me, and I took the opportunity to scoot as far away from him as I could.

"Not bad," Nina said, glancing at me. "Better for some people who don't have to work." She had a lot of nerve for someone who was late practically every night. I was getting fed up with her attitude.

"Everyone needs a night off," I said.

"Ain't that the truth," Marcus said. "So what have you been up to?" he asked Nina.

"I really have to go to the bathroom. See you guys later!" I grabbed my drink and practically sprinted away from the bar before Marcus could say anything else. I wished Cheryl would show up and take a look at the way Marcus and Nina were acting together. Maybe *that* would convince her he was a slimebag. I decided that Marcus really *was* just a garden-variety creep. And while I didn't like him and he freaked me out, and while I thought Cheryl shouldn't be dating him, I doubted he was really danger-ous. He kind of reminded me of Teddy, in a way. All bark and very little bite. Why were guys so evil like that? They all tried to be so tough—so badass. Hiro could have had Marcus on the floor in no longer than it took for him to blink an eye, yet—

No. I couldn't go around comparing every man to Hiro. And, as far as Marcus was concerned, there was no com-parison. Besides, my problems were starting to feel very far away. Almost like I was floating . . .

"Hey, are you okay?"

"Huh?" I opened my eyes and a blond girl with corn-rows was peering at me. *So Christina Aguilera,* I thought. Except the blond chick was wearing considerably more clothing, which wasn't saying much—she was, like, two degrees away from naked instead of one.

"It's just—you looked like you were going to be sick or something. And it's your turn."

What was she talking about? I felt fine. Maybe a little woozy, but that was because I was still catching up on sleep. I hadn't managed to nap that afternoon when I got home because I was still too wound up from my conversation with Karen—if you could call it a conversation. In fact, I felt great. I looked in the mirror while I washed my hands, then ran my fingers through my hair to get out some of the snarls.

Don't let Marcus ruin your night, I lectured myself. *This is your time to let go.*

When I reached out to grab my drink, which I'd balanced on top of the hand dryer, I knocked it into the garbage can.

"Oops." I giggled. "Bye-bye, Mr. Vodka!" The whole thing struck me as very amusing. I fished the glass out and set it gently against the wall under the sink. "Shhh . . . ," I said to it, holding my finger against my lips. "Don't tell anyone you're here." I laughed again and stood up. I was ready for more dancing.

Back outside, I stood for a moment in the shadows of the hallway that led down to the washrooms and the coatroom. Where was Marcus? I wanted to get back on the dance floor without having to deal with him again. I searched the club, sashaying a little to the beat of the music. My vision seemed kinda blurry. *Great,* I thought, *all those years at home and now, when I'm on my own, my vision starts to go.* I didn't have the slightest idea how a person went about getting a pair of glasses, but I was pretty sure it would be expensive. I squinted at the crowd.

"Excuse me," I said, tapping a girl with glasses on the shoulder. She turned around. "Can I borrow your specs for a minute?"

"What?" She stared at me like I'd asked her for some money or something.

"Your glasses, your glasses. Can't I just see them for a second?" She looked confused. "My vision seems to be blurred."

"You don't say?" she said, and turned away.

I stood up straight. Way to be so rude. I scanned the crowd again.

Marcus was coming toward me. First I spun around and headed back down to the bathroom, but that seemed stupid. I wanted to be out in the crowd, I *needed* to dance. I turned and headed straight for the dance floor. Mean old Marcus wasn't going to keep this girl down! Glasses or no, no sirree.

"Would you like to dance?" I flung my arm around the first cute guy I passed. I could see Marcus out of the corner of my eye. He was staring at me. *Eat your cheatin' little heart out, Marky Marcus!*

"With you?" the guy asked. He was a little short for me, maybe, but built.

"Yes, I do. I think. You remind me of a boy that I—once knew . . . ," I crooned, grabbing his hand and pulling him out of the shadows.

"You got it." He put his drink down on a nearby table.

"You mean yes?" I asked stupidly, stopping in my tracks. If he meant yes, then why couldn't he just say so? Why did people in L.A. have to be so *weird* about everything? Couldn't anyone just *relax?* He looked at his two friends, and they cracked up.

"Yes." He looked back at his friends. One of them gave him the thumbs-up. I dragged him toward the dance floor, ignoring Marcus completely, who I sensed was still staring at me. At us.

"What's your name?" I asked as I wrapped my arms around his neck.

"Keith. You?"

"Heaven."

"Really?"

I nodded. "Yes, it's my real name. It sounds different in Japanese."

Keith half smiled and wrapped his arms around my waist. "Well, you do look heavenly, that's for sure."

I secretly rolled my eyes. "You know, when I came to L.A., I resolved that I'd only date guys who didn't make stupid cracks about my name," I whispered to Keith.

"Who's talking about dating? I thought we were just having some fun."

"Bingo," I said, pulling him closer. Keith was kind of a cheeseball—he didn't really fit in at Vibe with his long dark hair and Guido clothes, but he was a good dancer. "Fun times for everyone!" I threw my arms up in the air.

"Now you're talking!"

So we danced. Songs came and went, and Keith and I just kept on going. He put his hand on my butt, and I left it there. His body was warm against mine. I closed my eyes, and the whole world seemed to spin away from me. I could have been out on the dance floor with anybody. It was wonderful to be able to forget like that.

"How about a break, Heavenly?"

I opened my eyes and nodded reluctantly. I never wanted to stop dancing. He led me back to the booth where his friends were sitting and sent one of them off to get drinks. I ordered two vodka cranberries. His friends ignored me—they were having some boring conversation about sports. I sighed, drumming my fingers against the table. Time was a wasting!

"Ain't no time like the present for a par-tay, know what I'm saying?" I said to one of the friends.

He stared at me.

"I'm just saying . . . ," I said, shrugging. I looked around and spotted Dubious walking past our booth.

"Hey, Dubious! My old friend! Whatsup!"

"Heaven?" Dubious turned around, and when he saw me, he looked like he'd just unwrapped a Christmas present. "Good to see you."

"Good to see *you*," I said, and actually meant it. "How's your night going?"

"Oh, you know. Same old same old. Where's your friend Cheryl?"

I shrugged. "Working, I think. She couldn't make it tonight. Bad luck for her because the party has start-ed! Wooh!" I slapped my hand down on the table.

"Christ," muttered one of the friends.

"No, Heaven," I said.

"Are these friends of yours?" Dubious whispered, leaning toward me.

"Oh, yes," I answered loudly. "This is—hey, what's your name again?" I reached over the table and tugged on the arm of the guy who'd called me Christ.

"Mark," he said shortly, and looked at his friend.

"Peter," said the other, and then they went back to talking, ignoring me.

"Aren't they sweet?" I asked Dubious. "These are some very nice boys."

"Uh, Heaven—are you okay?" Dubious looked concerned.

"Okay? Of course. I'm great! Isn't Vibe the best?" I jumped up and gave Dubious a hug.

"Um . . . yeah. I mean, I like it, but . . ."

Just then Keith came back to the table and put down my two drinks in front of me.

"And this," I told Dubious conspiratorially, feeling kind of sneaky, "is Keith. Now, *he* is special."

Dubious nodded at Keith, then crouched down next to me.

"Hey, Heaven. Maybe it's time for you to go home."

"What are you talking about? It's early. Why don't you join us?"

Dubious looked at the three guys and then back at me. "Why don't you come back to my table?"

Keith leaned over me. "Why don't you move along, brother? Heaven's fine. We're all just hanging out."

"Aw—Dubious," I wheedled, "why do you look so dubious? All is well, my friend. All is well. . . ." I stroked his cheek. He was such a sweetheart. A good friend. The best.

"Are you absolutely sure you're okay?" he asked me.

"I'm fine," I assured him. "I'll come visit you later. Cross my heart."

"Okay," Dubious said doubtfully, edging away from the table. "Be careful."

I laughed and waved good-bye as Dubious walked away. *Why so blue, Du?* I thought with a giggle.

"Isn't he a sweetie?" I asked Keith. "He's here almost every night. A real regular. We're pretty tight." I leaned closer to Keith. "Like this," I said, crossing my fingers and holding them in front of me. "Do you understand?"

Keith nodded, squeezing me even closer. "I got it. But how are *you?*"

"Excellent, thank you," I said, downing my drink. "Let's dance."

"You like those, huh?" Keith asked, ignoring me. I was sandwiched between him and one of his similarly buff friends.

"Thirsty," I said, and stared at the dancers, trying to think what else to talk about. What *did* people talk about at a place like this? With a random guy? Possibly best to keep my mouth shut. But there was so much I wanted to say! The craziest things . . . like: "When I was twelve, I had a little dog. I named it Koo Koo Roo." I giggled. None of it was true.

"What?" Keith asked, putting his hand on my thigh. Feeling good, I was feeling fine. I wanted to leave his hand there, and I did.

"Nothing—it's just—it's funny that I'm sitting here with you and we've only just met. I mean, you could be anyone. A gang member or something." I laughed.

"A gang member?" Keith laughed, "Actually, I'm a personal trainer from San Diego. How does that sound?"

"Sounds freaking excellent to me," I said. I did *not* need to be hanging out with any gangsters, nope, nope. "Do you train celebrities?" I asked, propping my chin in my hand on the table. "I really, *really* want to know."

"Some. Mostly just normal folks like you." Keith ran his eyes over my body. "You work out a lot, don't you?"

"Yep. Actually, I just left my trainer. So I'm in the market for another one," I said, flexing my arm in front of Keith's face. *Who said I wasn't a flirt? If Cheryl could see me now, she'd know I wasn't uptight. I was the* flirt master!

"Really?" Keith asked, massaging my leg. "I might be able to help."

"You might." I shrugged. I was aware of his hand on my thigh and the closeness of his body to mine, and it felt good. A tiny voice somewhere said, *Watch out.* I immediately told it to shut up.

"What kind of workouts do you do?" Keith asked.

"Martial arts. Karate. Jujitsu. Ninjitsu. Aikido. Some judo," I bragged.

"Wow? So you could kick my ass?" Keith pulled me closer.

"Probably," I said, and smiled. I could tell he didn't believe me, and that just seemed hilarious. "Hi-ya!" I said, giving him a soft karate chop to the shoulder. I dissolved into laughter.

"Why don't we go somewhere where you can show me some of your moves?" Keith said, bringing his face close to mine.

"Sounds good to me—how about one more drink?"

"You got it."

Keith brought me my drink, and I pounded it, dancing a little in my seat. Delicious. But Keith was getting boring. I needed some action. I felt like something *very exciting* would happen if I could only get back into the crush of the crowd, get lost in the dark corners of the club.

"I need some ak-shun," I said, laying my head on Keith's shoulder. "I'm getting so sleepy."

"Is it time to go?" Keith asked, running his fingers through my hair.

"Yep," I said, and stood up abruptly. It took a lot of effort. I edged out of the booth and banged my hip on the edge of the table—hard.

"You okay?" Keith asked. His friends had odd, smug looks on their faces.

"What are you looking at? Nothing to see here." I tried to look elegant. "I'm fine, Keith," I said, finding it hard to get my words out. "Which is more than I can say for your *friends*." My body felt mushy, and the room was spinning. Vibe effect! It was amazing what these clubs did to draw in the crowds. Keith grabbed my arm, and I concentrated on putting one foot in front of the other. On the way up the steps I stumbled again.

"Whoa! You're okay. Come on." Keith put his arm around my waist.

Suddenly a wave of nausea washed over me. I grabbed the railing and leaned my head against it. "You know what," I said, trying to sound alert and competent, "I'm thinking this isn't such a good idea. I'm pretty tired, so I think I'm just going to go home."

"Come on," Keith wheedled, trying to pull me onto my feet. "You were going to show me your moves."

"Yes, well, maybe some other time," I said with

exaggerated politeness. The railing was so cool against my forehead. "I'll be staying here right now. Catch you later."

"Uh-uh, honey, we're heading out." Keith hauled me onto my feet, and I lolled against him.

"So tired. Maybe next time . . . ," I muttered, concentrating on my toes. It seemed to help.

"Let's go, one step at a time." I half tried to pull his arm off from around my waist, but he wouldn't let go, and I had about as much strength left in me as a baby.

"I feel like a jellyfish," I said, "and why would you take a jellyfish from her home in the sea?"

"You'll feel better once we get out of here."

"But the sea . . . ," I moaned.

Keith pressed up against me in the darkened stairwell. I sensed his face moving toward mine, and I turned my head. He planted a kiss somewhere in the neighborhood of my ear.

"I could be poisonous," I muttered, flailing for the railing again. "You are endangering both our lives."

"Come on. Let me take you home, then. You're in no condition to go by yourself." He started up the steps again, dragging me next to him.

"Really, it's cool, Heath—"

"Keith."

"Keith. Right. Sorry. Ummm . . . just get me a cab." I felt like I was going to puke. This was wrong. All wrong.

"I'll get you home. Don't worry about it." Keith pushed open the door, and I tripped out into the open, panic rising in my throat. What was I doing? I really did feel like I was floating in a deep, dark watery space. "Do jellyfish puke?" I asked as the cool night air hit me.

"You okay, Heaven?" Matt the Bouncer slid off his stool—all six feet six of him—and grabbed me under my arms right as I was about to slide to the ground.

"Matt!" Relief rushed through me. I hugged him. "You are my friend," I said, "even if I am somewhat jellylike."

"Are you going to be sick?" I heard Matt ask, as if from far, far away.

"Um, Heath—I mean, Keith here was just going to help me get a cab." I clung to Matt, deeply comforted.

Matt stared at Keith. "Why don't you go get a cab, then?"

Keith cleared his throat, stared back at Matt, then took a few steps away and whipped out his cell phone.

"Cab's on the way," he said after a minute.

"Well," Matt said firmly, "I guess you got Heaven a cab. So you can go back inside now. Enjoy the rest of your night." Matt glared at Keith.

"Yes, enjoy," I said.

"Actually," Keith said nervously, "Heaven and I are planning on sharing a cab."

Matt looked at me. I shook my head. "I need to go home," I said. "Home."

169

"The lady's going home," Matt said, "you heard her. So why don't you just get back in there and try again?"

Keith shot one more look at me, then one at Matt, then banged back into the club, slamming the door behind him. I shut my eyes. My head was spinning.

"Thank you," I said to Matt. "I seem to have lost my bearings."

"You okay?" Matt asked, grabbing my arm just as I was about to keel over again.

"Too much to drink," I said. "I'm bad. Bad fish."

"Happens to the best of us," Matt said. "At least you were here, where you have people to look out for you."

The cab pulled up. I hugged Matt again. My savior. At least I had one true friend. I knew that now. No, two. Matt *and* Dubious.

"You sure you're going to be okay?" he asked. I nodded, trying to get my eyes to focus on Matt's kind face.

"Yep. Just gotta walk up the steps to my house and I'll be A-okay."

Matt slammed the taxi door after me, and I waved to him as we pulled away.

I pressed my head to the cool window, feeling excruciatingly sorry for myself. *I can't even do something crazy and stupid right,* I thought. I'd gone to Vibe alone to dance out my troubles, and all I'd managed to do was get drunk and end up running away from *two* guys. I was torn between two roles, samurai girl and regular girl—neither of which I was very good at. Limbo. I couldn't shake my past—and I sure as hell didn't have much of a future. I was just a worthless jellyfish, floating aimlessly among the sea creatures.

I fished in my messenger bag for a tissue, thinking about how Hiro confessed to having spoken with Mieko. Now it didn't seem so weird that he would have waited to tell me. I didn't appreciate him handling me with kid gloves, but deep down I knew he had my safety in mind. Hadn't he proved that again and again? But I'd become all moralistic about it—ready to pick a fight with him because fighting with him seemed better than living with the dull, aching knowledge that we could never be more than friends. When I yelled at him that day, I wasn't really thinking about Mieko—I was thinking about Karen.

The taxicab idled at a red light. Staring out the window through my tears, I saw that we were back in Hollywood, not far from home now, and that at the corner of the intersection there was a big, clean gas station. I used to stop in there all the time on my way to the dojo to stock up on Powerbars and bottles of water.

"This is fine," I said, hastily blowing my nose as I pulled cash out of my bag for the driver.

"You said Dawson Street," the driver said, sounding irritated.

"Yeah, sorry. I have to run an errand." I pressed a twenty into his hand, and waited anxiously for my change.

Now that I had made a decision, I didn't want to lose my resolve.

"You run an errand at two-thirty in the morning?" the driver asked.

I tried to think of a snappy comeback, but nothing came to me, so I just pocketed the change and hopped out, tripping on the curb. In the gas station convenience store, I bought an international calling card with enough credits for a ten-minute call to Japan.

When I got to the pay phone, a wave of nausea overcame me, and I leaned over and puked into the bushes.

Gross. After a few heaves my stomach was free of every last drop of vodka and cranberry juice. My throat burned, and I went back into the gas station for a bottle of water. This time the attendant definitely gave me the once-over. Outside, I sat on the curb and gulped the water down.

At least I could see straight now.

"The world has ceased to spin," I said out loud. More than anything, I wanted to be home in my bed. But I had to call.

For the second time that night I thought of my mission—to clear my mind. At that moment it seemed like calling Mieko was the one thing that might help me do that. I had to know what was going on in Tokyo. I had to face the unknown, no matter how scary or how upsetting it might be. *Heaven must be a strong, fighting samurai fish,* I said to myself. But I didn't find it very funny anymore.

I breathed a sigh of relief. "I will, Harumi-san. But not right now." I heard Harumi click her tongue with disapproval, and I could tell by her uncharacteristic silence that she was fighting tears, which made me want to cry all the more. "I miss you," I said softly.

"I'll get your mother," Harumi said, then, in a stage whisper, "please come home, Heaven-chan. It is necessary." She laid the phone on the table with a clunk before I could respond. I held the receiver, staring at my watch. Two minutes down, then three, then four. Where was Mieko? The card was running out of time.

Then suddenly that familiar dry voice that always reminded me of lizards came on the line. "Heaven? Is that really you?" I hadn't spoken to Mieko since just before the wedding ceremony, and hearing her voice was a shock. She sounded more forceful than I ever remembered her being. Mieko was, in general, cold and subservient. She lived a ghostlike existence in a quiet orbit around Konishi. The only life of her own she had was shallow and superficial, and she filled it with activities like shopping and ladies' teas. I doubted she would have bothered to leave the house at all if my father hadn't expected it of her. But now she sounded competent, strident—together. Maybe all that had happened had changed her as much as it had changed me.

"Yes, Mieko. It's me. How are you?" As soon as I started talking, I realized I had no idea what to say. What did I hope to learn from her?

As I dialed, I prayed Mieko would be at home. I knew that if I didn't reach her now, I wouldn't try again. The time was right . . . it would be 7:30 P.M. in Tokyo.

The phone rang four, five, six times. My heart was in my throat. Or maybe I just needed to barf again. Where were all the servants?

"Moshi moshi?" My eyes welled up again as I recognized the voice of Harumi, the loyal old nanny who had taken care of Ohiko and me growing up.

"Harumi-san?" I whispered her name. For a moment there was silence, then . . .

"Heaven! Heaven, daughter! Where are you? What are you doing? Are you alive?" Harumi yelled her questions into the phone as though she was speaking into a loudspeaker, and it was so loud that I had to hold the receiver away from my ear. She would never accept that telephones didn't require you to shout every word at the top of your voice. Ohiko and I had always teased her about it.

"Harumi-san, stop. I'm healthy. I'm well. I need to speak to Mieko."

"Heaven-chan, you must come home. You must come home and be with your family."

"My father—Konishi—is he . . . ?" I was afraid to hear her answer, but I had to know.

"Your father still sleeps," Harumi said shortly, "and you must come home."

"Never mind that," Mieko said. "Where are you?"

"I'm safe. I'm still in the States. Hiro told me that you called him."

"Are you living with him, Heaven? Hiro would not tell me where you were. He was most impolite on the phone."

"No, Mieko, I'm not." I tried to imagine the conversation between Hiro and Mieko—I was pretty sure Hiro hadn't been rude. It just wasn't in his nature. But Mieko didn't like being told "no" by anyone except Konishi. How much had Hiro actually said—did Mieko even know for sure that I was still in Los Angeles? If not, was it safe to let her know? "I'm in L.A.," I blurted, deciding I had to trust someone. Besides, gauging from my run-ins with the yakuza, my whereabouts were pretty common knowledge.

"Heaven, you must come home," Mieko said in what, for her, was a gentle voice. She even sounded anxious— could it be that she realized, for once, how important what was left of her family (i.e., *me*) was to her?

"I can't, Mieko. It's not safe. There are still people trying to harm me. I might endanger you and Konishi if I return."

"Your father is doing better, Heaven. We think that he will be coming out of his long sleep soon."

"Really?" I asked, surprised that Harumi hadn't mentioned that before. "Is that what the doctors say?"

"Yes. They are confident that he will awaken in the next

week or two. You must be here, Heaven. It will help him to recover when he hears your voice and knows that you are safe. You know how he loves you. You will give him the strength to fight."

I flashed back to the image of my father hurling himself at the ninja who'd interrupted our meeting in Little Tokyo. Konishi was injured trying to save me — I'd lost my katana, my long sword, and only my father's intervention had saved my life. I saw my father lying on the floor in a pool of blood all over again. If only I had refused to meet him that night at the restaurant in Little Tokyo! If only I had been a better fighter and not a scared little brat with only a couple of months of training under my belt! Maybe I owed it to my father to go back to Tokyo — or maybe it would only make matters worse. I leaned my head against the metal of the phone booth. Why was I always confronted by two bad choices? If I went back, I might lead another ninja straight to his bedside. If I stayed in the States, I might never see my father again — and there was no guarantee that I'd figure out who was trying to destroy us. Nothing was ever clear, nothing was ever easy. All I wanted to do was what was right — which was hard when all paths seemed equally wrong.

"Tell me where you are," Mieko continued. "I'll send you a ticket and money for the trip. You'll be home by the end of the week."

"I need to think about it," I said. What was I supposed

to do? What was the loyal, dutiful thing to do? "It may not be safe for me or for you," I repeated, not knowing how else to respond.

"Don't be ridiculous," Mieko snapped, a sudden edge in her voice. I pictured her standing ramrod straight next to the phone table, perfectly coiffed as always—Chanel suit, tasteful jewelry, hair freshly arranged by her private stylist. "You know your father's men can protect you better than this Hiro character, whoever he is. You have nothing to fear once you arrive in Tokyo. I'll see to that."

"They didn't protect Ohiko, did they?" I regretted the words almost as soon as they left my mouth. The one thing I knew for sure was that Ohiko's death was as devastating to her as it was to me. He was her *real* son, after all. Mieko sucked in her breath, and when she spoke again, her voice was strained.

"That was different." She paused. I waited for an explanation, but all she said was, "Please don't put yourself at risk, Heaven. Tell me where to send the money."

I looked down at my watch. One minute left. *Think, think,* I told myself. The prospect of flying back to Tokyo and potentially escaping this American nightmare was tempting. I'd see my father, maybe even help him to get better. On the other hand, if I left now, I'd never resolve things with Hiro—I'd be leaving Cheryl in the lurch with the rent. I'd be sheltered and protected just like I always had been. I'd be the old Heaven.

And the new Heaven still had a lot to figure out. Like who was responsible for Ohiko's death. And how Konishi's being a member of the yakuza fit into the puzzle.

"No, Mieko. I'm sorry. I'll call you again as soon as I can. But there are things I need to do here."

"Heaven, you're not thinking clearly. You must understand—"

"I understand. And I'm sorry. Please give my love to Konishi. I would come back if I could, but I can't."

"At least let me send you some money, then—you can decide later if you want to buy a ticket. Just give me your address," Mieko wheedled, starting to sound almost desperate. Why was she suddenly so eager to have me around? Just because it would win her points with Konishi when he woke up? It occurred to me suddenly that I'd never thought about what she stood to gain from all that had happened. It was too much to think about right now. But I had to trust my instincts. And they were screaming at me not to give myself over to the supposed security she offered.

"Not now—I have to go. I'm sorry, my time is running out." I gripped the phone tightly, leaning into the booth and closing my eyes. "I'm sorry, Mieko," I whispered.

"Heaven—don't be silly. You must tell me—"

Click.

The call ended. I slowly hung up the phone. For a million reasons that weren't entirely clear to me, I couldn't go home—but staying in L.A. seemed like a dead end. Vegas? That was a dream. I'd have to find Katie first.

I sighed. The truth of the matter was, I was hopelessly stuck.

I was also drunk. And alone. Another wave of nausea overcame me, and I leaned over the bushes again but could only manage a few dry heaves. When I stood up, some guy pumping gas into his SUV stared at me, then looked away in disgust. Great. If only Hiro could see me now.

Hiro had been right. I had to commit to my training—or to *something*. I couldn't go on living like this, without purpose, without peace. I shouldered my messenger bag and trudged toward home.

Limbo was a difficult place to be.

Dammit.

I think I miscalculated.

When I hung up the phone, I immediately called my brother, Masato, who thankfully remained in the United States after the wedding. He is seeing to things on that end, while I remain dutifully by my husband's side. He assured me that I had done my best, that there was really no pressing need for Heaven to set out for Tokyo right now.

"Heaven will return before long," my baby brother said. "That is certain."

Poor Masato. For so long he has been in exile, breaking his back to uphold the Kogo interests in South America— the Kogo empire is vast and has been built on the backs of those like my brother, who shed their sweat for it day in and day out. For Masato, this day has been long in arriving. But now he has a chance to finally help the family, and it is my duty as his sister, and as the wife of Konishi Kogo, to assist him in his leadership at this moment. In this time of difficulty we must help each other. And with my husband in his coma, who else can I trust? To whom should I turn?

I fear the Yukemuras, even if Masato believes they are a bunch of bumbling fools. They have wreaked havoc at every step. I pleaded with Masato to have them driven from Los Angeles—there are ways. I am silent but not ignorant. I know how these matters are taken care of. But Masato refused because he is brave. When his day of reckoning comes, he wants to enjoy it fully.

I hope he is right. I hope there is no danger.

Masato must be safe. I cannot afford to lose him.

The servants are in bed now, and only I remain awake, smoking one of the French cigarettes (which Konishi so disapproves of) in my darkened bedroom. Sometimes I smoke one even as I sit at his bedside. I wonder if he knows?

The smoke circles up into the darkness and fades away. A small part of me hopes that Heaven has found the freedom she craved when she lived here on the compound. Perhaps the American lifestyle suits her. I wouldn't be surprised. She was always a vivacious girl.

So unlike me.

I stub out my cigarette, watching the last embers burn themselves to ash.

Fate will bring what it will. It always does.

Mieko

I sat down at the coffee table with a cup of green tea and decided to make a list of all the things I should be doing. I had to take action. I'd hit my nadir—my lowest point, my wall. Things couldn't get much worse. So it was my job to make them better.

Number one was easy:

No more drinking! Clouds judgment. Not safe. Not even really fun. Embarrassing. (Remember: jellyfish.) Ends in puke.

Eat healthy.

Continue training on my own. Daily workout. Meditation. Get back in focus.

Work hard. Stop watching TV. Get on schedule.

Save money for own place.

Make things right with Cheryl.

Forget about Hiro. Move ON.

Make it right with Karen?

I looked over my list, thinking of specific things I could do to make each goal happen. Since I had the next few days off from Vibe, I knew I'd be able to get a jump start on my new "total lifestyle."

Some of the stuff was easy. The first thing I did was head out to the health food store and stock up on fruit and vegetables, brown rice, and lots of tofu. I needed protein and energy. I came home and set to work making a huge egg white omelette with tons of vegetables and wheat toast. Just as I sat down at the dining-room table with my plate (I didn't want to be tempted to flip on the television), Cheryl walked in the door.

"Hi," I said brightly, hoping yet again to break the ice. "I just made some breakfast. Want some?"

"It's a little late for breakfast, isn't it?" Cheryl said, without looking at me.

"Brunch, then." I tried to keep my voice even. I wanted to be back on good terms with Cheryl, but there was a limit to how many cutting remarks I could take. The fact of the matter was, Marcus *was* a jerk. And the way he'd acted last night (with me *and* Nina) proved it.

"No, thanks." Cheryl glided into her room and shut the door without another word. I closed my eyes and took a few deep breaths. I refused to let the Cheryl situation cloud my purpose. *This is day one, day one,* I repeated to myself. But number six on my list was going to be hard to achieve.

As I ate my eggs, I contemplated how best to manage the rest of my time. I had two days off, and I had to get back on track before returning to Vibe. I didn't want to be tempted into any sort of partying. I threw my dishes in the sink and pulled on my gym shoes. Time for number 3—workout. And maybe I could think of a way to deal with number 8—Karen—while I was at it.

After a brief stretch on the front lawn I jogged down Dawson Street, being extra careful of my breathing and my stride. I ran through a mental checklist of my body, which felt stiff at first but loosened up after a couple of blocks. My side was all but healed—it was still a little green where the bruise had been, but it wasn't tender anymore. I stretched my arms above my head, concentrating on the soothing in and out of my breath as I fell into the rhythm of the run.

I stayed on the side streets, zigzagging my way through the neighborhood. Soon I found myself headed for Barnsdall Park, where Hiro and I used to have our morning aikido workouts. I hadn't really planned on going that way; it just sort of happened. As I ran, I remembered the very first day of my training: how Hiro had woken me up at some horrific early hour and how surreal it had been to be standing there training with him—watching the mothers run by with their little three-wheeled jogging strollers, the yuppies walking their dogs. I'd dreamed of America for so long and seen so many images of it in the movies that I felt like I had stepped into one myself that day. Gradually, though, my surroundings began to feel real. I'd become even more American myself—my English was nearly flawless. I understood, for the most part, how the city worked.

Maybe I'd become *too* American. The more enmeshed I became in my L.A. life, the farther away I felt from Tokyo. Would I ever make it back to Japan? Would the American Heaven and the Japanese Heaven ever be able to coexist? I knew I had to find some sort of peace here, with or without Hiro.

I picked up my pace as the park came in view and collapsed on the nearest expanse of green to give myself a good stretch. My body protested at the long run, and my lungs felt a little raw. I'd have to get my endurance back up. I closed my eyes and lay on my back, pulling my knee up to my chest in a long stretch. The sun was warm but not hot— it was one of those beautiful California days that make you wonder why the whole world hadn't moved here. Seventy-six degrees. Zero humidity. A cool breeze.

Once upon a time in my life "before," Ohiko and I spent long days next to the gigantic swimming pool on my father's compound. My favorite month was April, when the temperatures were often warm but the thick humidity of the summer hadn't yet set in. The cherry trees that surrounded the lower end of the pool were covered in thick, white blossoms. We would always wait for the morning that the blossoms began to fall, and Yoshi, the pool man, knew to let them float in the water until they created a thick white blanket over the deep end of the pool. Then, one day, just before the last flowers tumbled to the ground, Ohiko and I would race to the pool and jump in. It was like swimming in perfume. I'd always put on my goggles and dive down to the very bottom of the pool, right next to the drain, then stare up at the surface, entranced by the way the sun cut through the blossoms. When we were very young, Ohiko and I would even pretend to be ships sometimes, fighting our way through the ice floes of the Arctic.

One day each year. After that, although we begged him to leave the flowers alone for a little longer, Yoshi would worry that Konishi would see them and be upset. My father had no time for such foolishness. He liked everything on the compound to be in perfect order, and he was not the type of man to understand the magic of a pool covered in blossoms or the excitement of a dive into that strange, shadowy world filled with beams of sunlight.

But Ohiko understood. He wasn't like the brothers in the movies I had seen—too bossy or overprotective or irritated by his little sister. When he learned something, he shared it with me, and when I was happy, he was happy. We grew up like two halves of the same person, and I never understood how it was that we didn't actually share the same blood. He felt like an extension of myself. Another limb that I'd come to rely on as much as if it had been a real, physical part of me.

Sadness welled up in my heart. My life had become so bizarre, so filled with anxiety and strange events, that I hadn't engaged in my usual daydreaming over the past few weeks. Even my dreams were empty.

I missed him. I missed my brother.

"Well, if it isn't Heaven Kogo."

My eyes snapped open. Karen's face loomed over me. Speak of the devil. I sat up quickly.

"Out for a little run, are we?" Karen said, propping one hand on her perfect hip. She was wearing a tank top and running shorts that left little to the imagination. *Be calm,* I said to myself, *this is your chance to make things right.* I didn't need any more enemies than I already had.

"Hi, Karen," I said, trying to sound as pleasant as possible, although my voice sounded forced even to me. "I'm glad I ran into you."

"And why is that?" Karen flipped the sunglasses she wore on top of her head down over her eyes. She wasn't going to make this easy.

"I wanted to say I'm sorry for how things turned out the other day at the dojo. I think we're both just a little stressed." I stood up, hoping to establish a more even footing for our conversation.

"That's an understatement," Karen said skeptically.

"So . . . ," I fished, "how are things going with you?"

"You mean, how are things going with me and Hiro, right? I mean, that's what you really want to know, isn't it?"

"N-No," I stammered, blushing. Why couldn't she take off those stupid sunglasses? "I was just asking. . . . I mean . . ."

"Everything is great, to tell you the truth." Karen smirked, pulling one leg up behind her in a runner's stretch. She was in total control of the conversation, and she knew it. "I think your fight actually turned out to be quite thera-peutic for him. He's far more relaxed now."

"Good to hear," I whispered. It felt like a stake was being driven into my heart. I wondered what, if anything, she'd told him about our argument. The thought that he might now hate my guts was appalling. I wanted to run away, but I forced myself to stay and hear her out. It was better to know everything. Then I could move on.

"We've even been talking about moving in together. It's a little early, but when things are right—you just know."

I nodded. *Can I just kill myself now?* I thought.

"You understand how it is, right? When you meet that perfect guy . . ." Karen tossed her head and stared off into the distance as though she was picturing all of Hiro's con-siderable assets in her head. "Something just clicks." She turned back to face me.

"Oh, I'm sorry," she said, her voice dripping with fake concern, "you've never really been with anyone seriously, have you? Well, you'll get there someday!"

I nodded again, not trusting myself to say anything. If this was how she was going to play it, then there was nothing I could do. I couldn't stand there and look at her anymore. It hurt too much. I took a deep breath.

"Okay. Great. Well, see you around." I grabbed my sweatshirt off the grass and tied it around my waist.

"You've got to go? I thought we could do a few circuits together, maybe." Karen grinned. She was truly evil.

"Maybe next time. See you." My face was burning as I jogged away, forcing myself not to sprint. The air around her was toxic, and I struggled to keep from crying as I ran out of the park and into a city where Hiro was dead to me forever.

I forced myself to keep running all the way home, even though my breath came in ragged gasps by the time I made it up the front steps. The house was silent. Cheryl had gone out again—no big surprise. Maybe I was the toxic one. My mind continued to race as I showered and changed into my gi pants and a tank top.

It was time to meditate. Just because Hiro was going to move in with Karen didn't make it any less imperative that I clear my mind and stay on the right path. Just because my heart was broken didn't mean I could give up. I might be alone, but I wasn't dead yet.

I spread a blanket on the floor of my bedroom and sat with my legs crossed and my hands on my knees. I breathed slowly in and out through my nose, using the techniques that Hiro had taught me way back in the day. At first, images popped up in my head like some kind of slide show on fast-forward. First the recent memories: Karen's angry sneer under the trees in the park, A. J. behind the bar at Vibe, flipping bottles and making change. Marcus's slow smile. Then further back—Hiro in his house the first time I saw him, when I showed up on his doorstep half dead from exhaustion and shock. My father's pale face when I held him after he'd been cut down by the ninja. Ohiko. Mieko sitting on the bed in my hotel room at the Beverly Wilshire, instructing me on what it meant to be a samurai bride.

Then the images slowed. I conjured a mental picture of myself in the pool at home and imagined that the scenes that filled my brain were cherry blossoms that I had to push aside in order to make a clear path through the deep blue water.

I swam and swam. My mind continued to slow.

You are a warrior, I thought. *A samurai. Nothing can change that. Not Hiro's love for Karen, not Cheryl's friendship, not your job at Vibe.*

You have to keep fighting.

I breathed deeply. The images were all still there, but now they lingered on the sidelines. I might not be able to get "empty," but at least I had an answer for now.

I opened my eyes and sighed. I'd known the answer when I woke up this morning, but now I was ready to accept it. It wasn't just that I was putting my life in order. It was *why* I had to.

I would keep fighting. For Ohiko. For myself.

1 2

"How about a drink, Heaven?" A. J. asked as I came behind the bar to refill my shot tray.

"No, thanks," I said as I squirted myself a Coke from the hand pump. "Soda's fine."

"Off the sauce, huh?" A. J. asked with a grin.

"Well, you know—I don't mix business with pleasure!" I laughed. I lined up shot glasses along the bar and decided to make what were called "Rock Lobsters." One part Chambourd, one part Grand Marnier, a finger of Crown Royal, and a dash of cranberry juice—the lobster in the rock. I was turning into a regular chemist behind the bar. The more ingredients, the better. A. J. pretty much let me decide which shots I was going to make as long as I mixed it up with every turn on the floor I did. When all the little lobsters were ready, I downed my Coke and headed back out.

Two girls stopped me for shots, laughing and chatting as they struggled in their bags for cash. It reminded me that I still hadn't made any progress on number 6 on my list— making things right with Cheryl. I'd still barely seen her, for one thing, and each time she'd been home, it was more of the same. She hadn't slept in her bed either night, and I really, really hoped she'd crashed with some other friend of hers and not with Marcus.

As if in answer to my thoughts, I felt a tap on my shoulder.

"Have you seen Marcus?" Cheryl's voice was cool, and she wouldn't look me in the eye. I tried to mask my surprise at seeing her. She'd avoided Vibe, too, since we stopped speaking. She was dressed in one of her trademark tiny skirts, and her hair was spiked up with gel—she'd shoved a big red hibiscus flower behind her ear, which clashed a little with her pink streaks. The look was very Kelly Osbourne meets—well, the eighties. But I had to give her credit— Cheryl had a gift for fashion. And she *always* stood out in a crowd. I suddenly felt dowdy in my black flared pants and motorcycle boots. I'd meant to go shopping for some new work clothes, but going alone hadn't seemed like much fun, so I'd just put it off. I guess secretly I was hoping that Cheryl would forgive me and we could go together. She knew all the best places.

"No, sorry," I answered, wishing that I had so at least I'd have something else to say to her. "How's it going?" I asked lamely. "Haven't seen you at home very much."

"I've been busy," Cheryl said offhandedly. I must have looked hurt because she quickly added, "Work. I've been pulling long shifts." It went against Cheryl's nature to be a total witch.

I nodded.

"Excuse me? Can we get our shots?" I turned back toward my two customers, and by the time I'd made change for them, Cheryl was gone. I scanned the crowd and saw that she had found Marcus and his pals, and they were all moving into a big booth. Marcus grabbed one of the waitresses and whispered what I could only hope was just his order in her ear. I noticed him run his hand down her leg, too. *What a scumbag,* I thought. Well, there was nothing I could do. Cheryl was a big girl. She'd have to fend for herself.

When I returned to the bar with my empties, A. J. waved me over.

"Heaven—you got a minute?"

"For you, ten." I was feeling more and more comfortable at Vibe these days, and it was second nature to tease A. J.

"Great—listen," A. J. said, wiping down the bar—he never stopped moving and was one of those people who could do twelve things at once and never even break a sweat, "We need a new bartender. Nina's quitting—"

"Quitting?" I asked, raising my eyebrows. Nina had never once been on time since I'd started working at Vibe, and I knew A. J. had probably had something to do with her "quitting." Not that I cared. She'd been nothing but a pain in my butt since I started at Vibe.

"Well—okay. She's been asked to resign. And since you said you'd be available for more shifts—how'd you like to take her place?"

I grinned. When A. J. had mentioned the possibility of me tending bar before, I'd thought he meant in about six months—not right away. But it would mean bigger money, and it would certainly be a lot more interesting. I'd have my own place in no time. Now that I was settling into this new phase, I was definitely willing to take on the responsibility.

"Is Nina still coming in tonight?"

"She was supposed to but . . . I don't think we'll be seeing her again."

"I'd love to!" I said, hoping A. J. was right and that I'd never have to see Nina again. I gave A. J. a hug. "Thank you so much!"

"Cool." A. J. looked pleased. And was he maybe blushing just a little bit? "Can you come in early tomorrow? I'll start going over the routine with you, and in a week or two we can put you behind the bar—we'll start off with slower nights so you can get your bearings, and after a month or so we'll start you regularly. No more slinging shots."

"Awesome!" I glowed as I prepared my next set of shots. Getting my attitude in place had improved things in every part of my life. Maybe now everything else would fall in line. Maybe.

Vibe was packed that night, and as I did my rounds, I couldn't help keeping an eye out for Cheryl. She looked serious, like she wasn't having the best time. I wondered if she was getting tired of Marcus. I steered clear of their table—I didn't want to ruin the good vibe (no pun intended) I had going on.

> *Check it out, check it out, hey, yo yo,*
> *I'm packin' cash like Konishi Kogo*

I froze in the middle of handing a bill back to a customer. They were literally playing my song. I glanced over at the bar, and A. J. gave me a thumbs-up. It was a little tribute to me. Thankfully, I didn't think anyone in Vibe would notice. Not a lot of Japanese people around. Instinctively I looked over at Cheryl.

As soon as I saw her, my heart shot into my throat. Trouble.

She and Marcus had separated from his group of banger friends and were standing against the wall in a darkened side of the club. They looked like they were arguing about something, and as I watched, Marcus grabbed Cheryl's arm. Cheryl pulled away and started gesturing. I could see she was yelling at him, and he was shaking his head, a deadly look on his face. I stared at them, frozen in place. It was as though everything else going on around me faded away, and all I could see was the two of them.

He pushed her back, and Cheryl stumbled. She looked shocked. Marcus got up in her face and yelled something, and Cheryl looked around, her face suddenly more pan-icked than angry. I swallowed hard and waited, not knowing what to do. Would Cheryl just hate me more if I tried to break it up? I contemplated getting Matt but couldn't decide. If I got the bouncer and nothing was wrong, then Marcus would *really* have it out for me. And Cheryl might never forgive me.

I put my tray down on an empty table, not taking my eyes off them. Marcus had grabbed Cheryl again, and this time she couldn't get out of his grip. In the next instant he spun her toward the wall, and I saw him raise his arm. Before I could stop myself, I yelled, "No!"

I saw the blow coming. He slapped her across the face. Hard.

The music swallowed my shout, and I felt weak for a moment, as though I was the one who'd been slapped. It was hard to believe what I was seeing. Cheryl raised her hand to her cheek in disbelief, and Marcus grabbed her around the waist and started dragging her toward the exit. Marcus ducked down and said something to his friends as they passed the table, and I saw him grab Cheryl's bag and jacket and shove them into her grip. She looked stunned— shell-shocked.

Suddenly the situation became all too real. I pushed my way through the crowd, trying not to lose sight of them.

Where the hell was he taking her? I came out on the other side of the dance floor in time to see Marcus drag Cheryl up the steps. Why was she going with him? Did he have a weapon?

Just before she disappeared up the stairway, Cheryl turned around. Her mascara ran down her cheeks in two dark streaks, and she had a wild look in her eyes.

"Cheryl!" I yelled.

She looked at me, then shook her head twice and mouthed the word, "No."

With another jerk she was gone, up the stairway.

I stood at the foot of the stairs, racked with indecision. What was I supposed to do? What *could* I do if Marcus had a gun? Would following Cheryl make things worse for her? Was she still so angry at me that she didn't want my help? *Don't be an idiot, Heaven,* I told myself. *You just saw him hit her. She needs you.* End of story.

I ripped off my apron and ran back to the bar.

"A. J.—I have to take a break—I'm sorry—there's an emergency." I shoved my wad of bills into his hand and grabbed my sweatshirt from where I'd stowed it under the bar. I scrabbled through my bag, looking for one of the switchblades I'd pocketed from the muggers. I'd been carrying it around with me since the night Cheryl and I were attacked. I wasn't a knife fighter—I'd trained with the katana, but knife fighting was a whole different ballgame. You had to get far closer to your opponent if you wanted to do any damage. I palmed the knife and slipped it into my sweatshirt, hoping A. J. didn't see what I was doing. I wasn't about to head out without some kind of protection.

"What? What's going on?" A. J. looked half concerned and half irritated.

"I've got to run, A. J. I'm sorry. I'll be back as soon as I can. You know I wouldn't go unless I had to."

A. J.'s expression changed to one of total concern. "Do you want me to call Matt?"

"No, thank you—I . . ." I knew I couldn't tell him what was going on. "It's just some personal stuff, A. J." Would I ever be able to be honest with *anyone?*

"Heaven—wait . . ."

But I couldn't wait anymore. Cheryl needed me. I vaulted up the stairs, past Matt on his bar stool, and headed into the night. I wasn't going to let another person I cared about get hurt.

That much I knew.

1 3

I burst out of Vibe and plowed through the group of people waiting in line to get in.

"Hey!"

I ignored the catcalls and shouts and made it out onto the street just in time to see Cheryl and Marcus rounding the corner. I sprinted to the end of the street, flattened myself against the side of a building, and peered around its edge. Marcus was dragging Cheryl along—it looked like wherever they were going, they were going on foot. I took a deep breath and focused, ready to slip into shinobi-iri—the ninja "invisibility" skill that I'd mastered when Karen was kidnapped. It was hard to explain exactly what I did to get myself into that invisible space—it was a trick of the mind and body that defied definition. All I knew was that I could feel my body adjusting to the change just like I was slipping

on a comfortable old coat. I slid down the street after them using "sideways walking," letting the shadows dictate my progress. Anyone watching wouldn't have seen me—just the outline of a dark shape out of the corner of the eye, a flicker in the darkness—a momentary disruption in the streetscape.

The dim, widely spaced streetlights worked both for me and against me—they gave me more shadows in which to slink, but I had a hard time keeping Cheryl and Marcus in view. We were heading deeper into the industrial part of town, and I registered that I was losing my bearings.

Suddenly Marcus and Cheryl stopped. I shrank back into the cover of a metal fire escape, straining my eyes for a better view. Cheryl was struggling against Marcus now, fighting him. I held back, every particle of my being wanting to go out and help her, but knowing that I had to get a better read on the situation before I could.

Marcus grabbed Cheryl under the arms and dragged her down the street. Cheryl kicked fiercely, and I saw Marcus grab his shin. *Stop, stop,* I telegraphed mentally, trying to send my brain waves out to Cheryl. *You're just making him angrier.* Cheryl fell out of Marcus's grasp for a moment, but her high-heeled boots slipped and skidded on the ground, and she fell to her knees. He hauled her up again, and they moved forward.

I needed help. If there was one thing I'd learned, it was that going into a situation like this one without backup could be deadly. I stayed as close as I dared, and after another block I found a pay phone. I picked up the receiver. The line was dead.

I scanned the street and saw there was another phone on the opposite corner. But to get there, I'd have to leave the shadows. Marcus and Cheryl had stopped, and Marcus was using one hand to talk on his cell phone and holding Cheryl around the neck (with his hand over her mouth) with the other. Cheryl had stopped fighting for the time being. I waited until Marcus turned away and then I lunged across the street, rolling and ducking into an alleyway on the opposite side.

Marcus turned around, and I held my breath. Had he seen something?

No. They turned the corner.

Without thinking, I grabbed the phone. A dial tone. I fished some change out of my pocket and dialed Hiro's number. *Please be home, please,* I prayed. I had no idea what Karen's number was. Hiro was my only hope. Seconds ticked by . . .

"Hello?" Hiro's groggy, muffled voice came on the line. I shook with relief.

"Hiro—I need you. Cheryl's in trouble, and I don't know if I can take care of it alone," I whispered.

"What?" Hiro sounded confused. "I can't hear you."

I raised my voice as much as I dared and tried again. "I just—listen—I can't explain everything right now. But I need your help. I'm at"—I paused, squinting at the street signs—"Cesar Chavez and Alameda. Right by the freeway—but heading north."

"Do. Not. Move," Hiro said, and I could hear him rustling around—probably throwing on his clothes. I couldn't help wondering if Karen was there. "I'll be there soon."

"I can't stay here, Hiro," I said. "I have to follow them."

"Stay," Hiro said, and clicked off. I slammed down the phone. If anyone could find us, it was Hiro. I ran off, hoping that I hadn't lost Cheryl and Marcus. No—they were moving underneath the highway. I skirted from column to column, trying to ignore the rumbling of the traffic overhead and stay focused. I felt trapped in some nightmarish cityscape right out of *The Matrix*. I scooted along a chain-link fence, using the heaps of piled-up building materials as a shield, and tried to keep Marcus and Cheryl in view. They'd crossed under the highway.

That's when I realized—they were heading for Union Station. The question was, why?

A few taxis still idled in front of the huge, stucco building, which looked like it had been lifted right off a movie set of Los Angeles circa 1925. I knew from the guidebooks I'd read about the city when I first arrived that the building was a sort of landmark, although I'd never seen it in real life. It was decorated with Spanish-style tiling and looked more like some of the mansions up in the hills than a train station. Was Marcus taking Cheryl on a train out of town? I doubted there was anything pulling out at two-thirty in the morning, although the station did seem to be open. Marcus and Cheryl were moving more quickly now, and the busy street and noise allowed me to follow them much more closely. Just as I thought they were definitely heading for the main entrance, Marcus made a sharp left and veered around toward the side of the building. My mind raced. I had to be prepared for anything—but I had no idea what I was headed for. If Marcus wanted to get Cheryl alone, to hurt her in some way, then why would he risk coming back out into the open like that?

The answer was simple. He was going underground.

I watched in horror as Marcus pulled Cheryl down into the steps of the subway station. I'd never been in L.A.'s system, but I knew from my few experiences riding the TRTA—Tokyo's subway—and from taking the Metro in Paris that subway stations were not optimal for fights. Narrow platforms, winding transfer passageways, and lots and lots of crowds. It would be insane for me to go down there.

But what could I do? Cheryl needed me.

I ripped off my sweatshirt and draped it over the metal railing that guarded the stairwell, praying that Hiro would see it. If he did, I knew he'd recognize it because I'd worn it practically every day during my first few months in the city. It was one of the only pieces of clothing I'd had, besides a pair of jeans and a few T-shirts. I felt in my back pocket for the switchblade. It was still there, and the feel of it comforted me. A little.

I slid down the steps, concentrating on making my footsteps as light as a cat's. The ceilings were high in the station, and I could hear Marcus and Cheryl arguing before I was even down the stairs.

When I reached the bottom of the steps, I saw that a metal grating had been wrenched open, and several padlocks hung loose from the twisted metal. The subway was closed—I remembered then how Cheryl had told me that the subways in L.A. closed at night.

I made my way past the ticket vending machines and stopped. Everything was quiet now. I looked around desperately, wondering why some helpful policeman didn't appear or even some homeless guy who was looking for somewhere warm to spend the night. But no—I was alone, except for Cheryl and Marcus. And it looked like I'd have to take on this problem myself.

I took a deep breath and strode out onto the platform, abandoning my invisibility. I could summon it again if I needed to, but right now I wanted to get a clear, total image of the space I was dealing with.

The platform was deserted. Cathedral ceilings soared over the empty tracks, giving the station the feel of some kind of futuristic church. Wooden benches lined the platform, which was wider than I'd expected.

"Matta attane," uttered a deep voice, in flawless

Japanese. *So we meet again.* I whirled around, expecting to see another yakuza hit man, maybe even the same guy who'd come after me before.

I froze. Marcus was standing about twenty feet down the platform, holding Cheryl in front of him, a knife to her throat. I looked wildly around—had that voice actually come from him?

"Hey, Heaven," shouted Marcus in perfect Japanese. "Your mother says hello." He stepped slowly toward me, still holding Cheryl in front of him like a shield.

I gasped. The first thing I thought was, *It was him,* and cursed myself for not obeying my intuition about Marcus. I'd known from the get-go that something was off about him, but I'd chosen to believe that he was harmless, just another creep. When would I ever learn my lesson? It wasn't the first time I'd ignored all the signs of danger that the samurai part of me was learning to sense—but I vowed then and there it would be the last. *If I get us out of this alive,* I thought, *I will never deceive myself again.*

Then I thought, *What did he say about my mother?*

"What are you talking about?" I yelled.

"Didn't you hear me?" shouted Marcus, in English this time. "I said Mieko says hello."

"Usotsuki," I hissed. Liar. But was he? How did he know Mieko's name? How had he managed to master such perfect Japanese? I'd been speaking English since I was a kid, and even I still had a slight accent. And *did he really know*

207

Mieko? My heart sank. I had a feeling that the next few minutes would change everything.

Cheryl whimpered, and Marcus covered her mouth.

"Let her go!" I yelled.

Marcus looked at me, then down at Cheryl. "Okay," he said, and hurled her away from him toward the wall. Cheryl slammed against it and slipped to the ground. Two of Marcus's banger friends I recognized from the club came out from behind him, and one of them grabbed Cheryl and pulled her back to her feet. She looked only half conscious and confused.

"Heaven, I'm sorry! I didn't know! I didn't know!" she shrieked. Her captor clamped his hand down on her mouth and laughed.

"She really didn't," said Marcus, all traces of the smooth player now gone from his demeanor. His voice was filled with hatred. "But now she does."

I heard a noise behind me, and I stepped back. Two more thugs. I backed toward the wall, trying to keep my vision on both pairs of men. As far as I could tell, Marcus was the only one who was armed. But I wasn't going to count on it. I felt scattered and lost, unable to formulate an attack. Could Mieko really be behind all this? Was that why she'd wanted my address? I couldn't stop thinking about the fact that Cheryl had been used by Marcus just to get to me. I was responsible for her being with him. It was all my fault.

Marcus and his men were closing in. I had only one choice—to take his knife away from him. I took a giant leap toward Marcus and threw myself into the air, launching a spinning kick at the hand that held the knife. I connected well and heard the knife clatter to the tile floor. But I misjudged my landing and ended up almost right at their feet. I sensed the other two coming from behind, and I somersaulted toward the edge of the platform, jumping to my feet just before going over. I was in a precarious spot—the worst place to be.

I dove forward onto the ground, flipped over, then clamped my legs around one of the meatiest attacker's ankles and knocked him to the floor with one quick wrench. Another roll and I was safely back from the edge of the platform. I arched my back and flipped myself onto both feet, assuming the ready position. I was in the zone. I whipped the switchblade out of my pocket and flicked it open.

Bring it on.

For the next minute there was no Heaven, no Cheryl, no fear, and no world outside the world of my own body, which moved as if on autopilot. I saw the attacks coming and dodged them. I grabbed an arm as it came toward me and pulled, wringing the wrist and sending its owner sprawling to the floor. I crouched down and sideswiped a leg, hit someone's neck with the side of my hand, kicked and punched and hurtled and flew and *fought*. These guys weren't fighters, but they were big and sturdy—more like tanks. I used the knife for a few opportune slashes, but I knew better than to rely on it completely. It was a good deterrent but little more. I was on fire. *I will put them down,* I told myself. *I will vanquish my enemy.*

"Momma didn't tell me her little girl could fight like this," Marcus hissed.

At that I crumbled. Marcus might as well have clobbered me on the head. Mieko, my adoptive mother, the only member of my family who was still in a position to help me, *had betrayed me.* And if she had sold me out, then did that mean she had abandoned Ohiko, too? Did it mean that Konishi was even now in danger from those who were closest to him? Did she have anything to do with his extended coma? Or was Konishi guilty after all, as I had believed at the start, when I saw him watch the ninja who killed Ohiko and do nothing?

I wanted to scream, to let out a howl of pain. *This can't be happening,* I thought, *Oh, please, just let this not be happening.* It was the worst moment I'd had since the night of the wedding. The knowledge that Mieko was out to harm me, in whatever way, for whatever reason, killed another little part of me. It seemed to me I could feel that last little bit of innocence slide away. And I wanted it back.

"I want it back!" I screamed, stumbling forward. Marcus looked confused for a second. I fought through my anger and delivered three hard punches to the solar plexus of the nearest banger, stupidly leaving my back open to attack. It was no use. My concentration was shot.

As soon as I had that realization, a huge force barreled down on me from behind. Before I could react, my arms were pinned down at my sides, and I was lifted off the ground.

"If you had just played nice the other night at the club, you could have made my job *a lot* easier. But you had to go flirt with your little dance boy." Marcus's stale breath made me gag. I whipped my head back, hoping to smash Marcus in the nose with the back of my skull, but he was too quick for me. Marcus squeezed my wrist so hard, I felt like my bones were about to snap, and the switchblade tumbled from my grasp.

"Now, now." He laughed. "Don't make this harder than it has to be."

I kicked as hard as I could, but Marcus's arms were like a vise. One of the other goons came over and grabbed my legs. They walked me to the edge of the platform.

"One," the goon said, grinning.

"Two," Marcus hissed, gloating.

"Three!" they yelled together, and dumped me over the edge.

Somehow I landed on my back right on top of one of the rails. The wind rushed out of my lungs with a whoosh and I rolled into the middle of the track, gasping at the searing pain that coursed through my body. I could hear their laughter and Cheryl's screams as if from far, far, away.

Air, air, air. I knew it would come back eventually, but it was hard not to panic. After what seemed like an eternity, I gobbled down a first breath with a rush and hauled myself onto my knees. Being without breath was the worst feeling in the world and one I seemed to be having a lot lately. When I looked up, I saw that Marcus and two of his cohorts were standing on the platform's edge, looking down at me, knives gleaming in their hands. Marcus held two—and one of them was mine.

I'd let my weapon fall into the hands of the enemy. Big mistake.

That's when I felt the ground tremble.

Marcus grinned.

A train was coming.

I staggered to my feet in time to see the bright pinpoint of light swelling into view in the dark tunnel. My back ached, and my head felt like it was about to explode. *Why is the train coming? The subway is closed!* In another second I had my answer—it was a maintenance train, a sort of flatbed truck of the rails, and it wasn't slowing down.

Marcus and his gang were blocking my only escape. I looked at them and then at the approaching train, whose bright orange front I could now see barreling toward me. The driver honked, and the sound reverberated through the station at a deafening volume. It felt like the whole world was shaking.

Marcus threw back his head and laughed, and I thought, *Not this way*. The first samurai lesson I'd learned was to accept death—and I was ready to die. Really, I was. But not without a fight. The train loomed closer, the noise grew louder, and the last thing I registered was the bobbing hard hats of the two subway workers who rode the train and who were gesturing wildly at me to clear the tracks.

And then . . . it all faded away. Just like that. The train seemed to shrink into itself until all that was left was a throbbing globe of light. A second globe floated where Marcus had stood at the edge of the platform. And the third globe rose straight out of my body, seemed to pour right out of my chest like those soap bubbles children blow through tiny plastic hoops—it hovered right in front of my eyes. As I watched, the three globes came together in front of me in one glimmering, shimmering, gleaming sphere. The sounds of the train, of the station, of Marcus's laughter—they all faded away. I had found my peace.

I bent my knees and hurled myself toward the sharp concrete edge of the platform. My fingers clamped down on the edge, and I channeled every iota of strength I had into pushing my body up into a headstand. In just one second I was clear of the tracks and without a moment to spare. A warm burst of air blew through the station, and a fraction of a moment later the train was rumbling by like some sort of fire-breathing dragon. I caught an upside-down glimpse of it just before I let the propulsion of my jump flip me all the way over back onto my feet. Without losing my momentum, I leaned back and delivered a kick to the chin of the nearest goon. His head snapped back. Another kick, this time from the left, and his knife fell down onto the tracks.

I dove behind them and jumped to my feet, planting another kick right in the lower back of the banger in the middle. He plowed into the train as it sped by and bounced back onto the platform. I caught a glimpse of his bloodied face as he struggled to his knees.

I knew I had to get rid of their weapons. It was my only chance. Marcus took a step back, and I ignored him while I took care of Heavy Number 3, who lunged toward me. I grabbed his hand and snapped his wrist with one crack, holding his limp arm in front of me as I spun into his grasp— a vicious tango. I heaved his damaged arm over my shoulder, delivered two sharp punches to his nose with the back of my hand, and flipped him over onto his back. He went down hard, but he went down.

I panted, looking around for Marcus—there. He approached me slowly, and I ignored the pain that coursed through my hands, my back, my legs as I prepared to take him down. The globe of light that had led me back into action was fading now. I knew I had to act quickly, or I'd be too spent to take Marcus down.

And I really, really wanted to take him down.

"Heaveeeeeeeeeeeeeeennnn!" Cheryl screeched. At the same moment I registered a dark shape running down the platform toward me in my peripheral vision. Marcus turned his head. *The fourth thug,* I thought. *There were four of them.*

I took two steps toward Marcus, hoping to finish him off before the fourth man got there, but suddenly the black shape was upon us.

Marcus crumpled to the floor.

Hiro. He'd flown across the platform like Jet Li—I would never have believed someone could travel so far in the air and still get so much force out of a kick.

Hiro landed beside Marcus just as he fell and delivered a quick chop to the back of his neck, finishing him. Marcus was down for the count.

We looked at each other. And that look seemed to say it all.

I stood over Marcus, hatred coursing through my body. I kicked him as hard as I could in the kidneys; he groaned, and lay still. I leaned over him, and whispered, "That's what you get for hitting a girl, you piece of crap."

"Heaven," Hiro said, putting his hand on my shoulder, "that's enough."

"Cheryl," I whispered hoarsely, looking around. She was being dragged toward the station steps, this time by Marcus's little henchman. Hiro and I sprinted over just in time to see Cheryl get in a kick. *Good for her,* I thought. Her captor doubled over, and Hiro went in to finish the job. I grabbed Cheryl and pulled her out of harm's way, then crouched at a safe distance in case Hiro needed backup. He didn't.

"Heaven, are you okay?" Hiro cupped my face in his hand, and the sweetness of his touch brought back the truth of how much I'd missed him.

"Yes. No. Yes." I closed my eyes for a moment, giving myself up to those two cool hands.

"You're going to have a terrible black eye," he said, running his hand lightly over my cheekbone.

"How did you find us?" I asked.

"Well, when you said you gave me the address, I figured that you were headed toward Union Station. And when I ran over here, I saw the sweatshirt—and heard the commotion."

I shook my head. "I knew you would," I said.

"Heaven?" Cheryl reached out from where she sat huddled behind me and tugged on the back of my shirt like a little kid. Her voice quavered.

I turned around and pulled her into a bear hug.

"I'm so sorry," Cheryl said, "Heaven, I really didn't know."

"I know you didn't," I said, "and I'm sorry, too."

"For what? I'm the jerk in this scenario." Cheryl wiped her eyes.

"I'll explain later," I said, and gave her another little squeeze. When I turned back to Hiro, his eyes were shining.

"We have to get out of here," he said.

"That's an understatement," I answered. I stood up, fighting to keep my legs from trembling. I offered Cheryl my hand, but when she stood up, a grimace of pain crossed her face.

"What is it?" I asked, grabbing her under the shoulders as she tottered.

"My ankle," she breathed, "I think I sprained it."

Hiro knelt down and eased off Cheryl's stiletto boot. She winced as he prodded her ankle. It was twice its normal size.

"Definitely sprained," Hiro said. "Come on—we've got to get you to an ice bag." Cheryl smiled wanly. We draped her arms around our shoulders and helped her up the stairs. I had a feeling that was as close to riding the L.A. metro as I was ever going to get. And that was just fine by me.

1 4

"I swear I had no idea, Heaven," Cheryl gasped, hopping between Hiro and me on her good leg. Hiro and I half supported, half carried her to the taxi stand in front of Union Station. "I really didn't think Marcus wanted to hurt you."

"It's okay, Cheryl," I soothed, "don't be silly. I didn't know, either."

"No, but you tried to warn me about him. And you were right—I should have thought twice about dating someone like that."

"Forget it," I said. "Please believe me. I'm not mad at you." Anger was the farthest thing from my mind. I felt more like someone had just run my body through a washing machine. I was ready to sleep for a month.

"I just feel so *stupid*," Cheryl said, her voice trembling. "And I've been such a bitch to you over the last week."

I stopped short and turned Cheryl toward me. "Stop it, okay? I'm just glad you're safe."

"I really want to make it up to you," Cheryl said, wiping her eyes.

"Great. You can make me dinner every night this week. How's that?"

Cheryl smiled a little. "If that's what you want . . ."

"Guys, come on," Hiro prodded. "We've got to get Cheryl home immediately."

"Oh, crap," I said as we hobbled the last few feet to the taxis. "I forgot my bag at the club."

"Can't you pick it up tomorrow?" Hiro asked.

"I really can't. Half the stuff I own is in that bag—and besides, what if Marcus and his friends go back there looking for me?"

Cheryl drew in her breath quickly, and I squeezed her shoulder. "We're almost there," I said, "hang on."

"It's not that—" Cheryl said.

"You're right. It won't be safe," Hiro interrupted, his brow furrowed.

I shifted my hold on Cheryl. "What's the big deal? I'll be in and out in one second. I—"

"I can't go there," Cheryl chimed in. "I don't mean to be a pain, but I think some of Marcus's friends might still be there. Please."

"You can just wait in the car," I said. "They won't even know you're there."

"No, she's right," Hiro said, "If they see you or Cheryl, they're going to wonder what went wrong. And who knows how many connections he has at that club? Besides, Cheryl needs to get ice on that ankle *immediately.*"

Cheryl nodded and added, "It's not safe, Heaven. Marcus knows *everybody.*"

I sighed. My brain was too tired to concentrate on the details of this tiny logistical problem after all that had happened. My moment of clarity felt long gone. I was paralyzed by indecision.

"Hiro," I said weakly, "just please do whatever you think best. But I need to get that bag."

"Do you think you can make it home on your own if we put you in a cab?" Hiro asked Cheryl, bending over to take another look at her swollen ankle.

Cheryl nodded gamely. "Of course. It's only a few steps to the door. I'll be fine."

"Are you sure?" I asked. I felt bad leaving her to fend for herself, but it seemed like the only reasonable way to get us all where we needed to be. Hiro went over to one of the cabs and leaned in the window to talk to the driver.

"Yes, I'm sure," Cheryl said. "I'm not a *total* wimp, you know."

"I know. You got in a few good hits back there."

Cheryl smiled. "I did, didn't I? I mean, nothing compared to your Michelle Yeoh *Supercop* action . . . you know that scene where she's riding on top of the car and—"

"Ha!" I interrupted her. I was no Michelle Yeoh, and I knew it. "I wish. I suppose you think Hiro looks like Jackie Chan?"

Cheryl wrinkled her nose. "Uh-uh. He's *serious*—more like Johnny Depp meets Bruce Lee." Cheryl lowered her voice. "Heaven—he's *really* hot."

"Tell me about it," I whispered, feeling my cheeks growing warm. "Bruce Lee wasn't Japanese, though," I teased.

"Duh. But you know what I mean."

I did. Watching Hiro fight was one of the most beautiful things I'd ever seen. He was so graceful and fluid—weightless, almost.

"Okay," Hiro said, returning. I hoped he hadn't overheard any of our conversation. "I've spoken with the driver, Cheryl. It's all paid for—he's going to walk you into the house, too, okay? So just go inside and put some ice on your ankle, lock the door, and we'll be a few minutes behind you. Just wait on the couch."

"Such a gentleman," Cheryl joked, widening her eyes at me. She wasn't the type to abandon humor for long. Hiro and I placed her gently in the backseat of the cab and watched her speed off before hopping into another one by ourselves.

"That was it!" Hiro said excitedly as our car pulled away from the curb.

222

"What?" I asked. I was acutely aware of how one of his arms was stretched over the top of the seat behind me. Our knees were touching. Hiro grabbed my hand.

"You did it! You cleared your mind."

I nodded slowly but couldn't manage to work up the same excitement as Hiro. The adrenaline that had pumped through my body had totally ebbed away, and I felt dull as an old coin. Hiro let go of my hand. I fought the urge to put my hand back in his.

"I suppose," I said with a sigh, seeing again for a moment the three luminous spheres that had guided me and feeling acutely the absence of his hand on mine.

"You suppose—Heaven, you were amazing! I told you before I thought you had natural talent—more than I've ever seen in one person. You can't deny your gift. You have to continue your training."

"Wait," I said, confused, "you mean you saw what happened on the tracks?"

"I came down the stairs just as the train was coming into the station."

I shuddered. "Close call, huh?"

"Yes, yes, it was." Hiro looked into my eyes, and I felt my heart melt. Everything that had happened between us seemed irrelevant. I forgot the fights, his not telling me about Mieko's call (and he'd turned out to have had the right instinct on that one, horrifyingly enough). And I concentrated on the fact that we were together. "Heaven," said Hiro, running his fingers through his hair, which was a little wilder than usual from all the action, "will you let me train you again? Can we get back on track somehow?"

"Yes," I breathed, afraid to let the goofy smile that was in my heart spread across my face. It was a good omen that he'd said what he had. *Back on track.* Exactly where I'd been trying to get myself over the last few days. And what was the use of pretending anymore? I loved him. What's more, I trusted him. And now he was the only one I had.

"But . . . ," I said. I had to ask. "Won't it cause problems to be training me if you and Karen are living together?"

"What?" Hiro pulled away and stared at me. "Who told you that?"

"Well, are you?"

Hiro looked embarrassed. "No. No way. That would be a little premature, don't you think?"

"I guess." I smiled to myself. So Karen had been lying. Could this moment get any better? "Hiro—there's something you should know."

"Tell me." Hiro moved closer, and we sat huddled in the middle of the seat with our knees touching and our faces close. Closer than we'd ever been, actually, except when we were sparring.

Just then the cab pulled up about a block from Vibe. Hiro jumped out.

"I'll be right back."

"Wait—Hiro—" Hiro turned around and ducked his head in the window.

"Do you need something?"

"Just—could you just tell A. J.—he's the bartender—tell him I'm sorry."

Hiro looked at me probingly, and his brown eyes seemed to go a shade darker.

"Okay," he said simply, and headed into the club. I watched his tall, lean body jog down the street and toward the front door. It was getting near closing time, and the crowd of people waiting to get into the club had all either gained entry or given up and gone home. It was hard to believe I'd never be going inside Vibe again—and I wondered if I'd ever see A. J. and Matt, or DJ Slavo, or even Dubious. It seemed a shame to meet so many people and then abandon them without so much as a good-bye. I'd been doing too much of that lately.

The mistake was thinking that I could build a home here, I thought. It was just impossible. Someone had already destroyed my home, destroyed my family, and I wouldn't be able to settle down anywhere until I figured out why. Because it looked like now I knew who was behind it. I closed my eyes and opened my mind to the information I had learned.

Mieko.

What could she possibly gain from killing me? Not

money, certainly. Her future was assured. Whatever happened to Konishi, even if he lived and if, in some bizarre tabloid twist of fate, he decided to divorce her, she would be okay for the rest of her life. She could be assured of living like a queen. And there was *no way* she had wanted Ohiko dead. He had been her only reason for living, as far as I could tell. So *what?* Was she caught in somebody else's grip? Was she being threatened by the yakuza—were they using her as a pawn? Or had she just been playing dumb all these years?

Hiro jumped back in the cab and gently handed me my messenger bag.

"Your friend A. J. seemed pretty concerned," Hiro said.

"He was a good friend," I said softly, looking Hiro straight in the eye. There was a deep connection between us—I knew Hiro understood what I meant. And I wasn't worried that he would think something had happened between A. J. and me. A week ago I might have enjoyed trying to make him jealous. But all that stuff just seemed petty now.

"What were you going to tell me?" he asked gently.

I told him about Marcus. About what he had said about Mieko. About his flawless Japanese. I told him about Teddy.

"I just don't know what to think," I finished, "I mean, it's the last answer I expected out of all this."

"More like just another question," Hiro said.

"You know what I mean—but *Mieko?* She was always such a *nonperson* at home. So submissive. And one thing I know for sure is that she loved Ohiko. He was everything to her. So how could she be this devil woman all of a sudden?"

"Looks can be deceiving," Hiro said mildly. He seemed much less surprised about the Mieko connection than I was, but then again, he didn't know her. He hadn't grown up in the same house with her.

"But they shouldn't be," I said, looking out the window. "When am I going to learn that I can't take anything for granted anymore? The only thing I'm sure about right now is you."

Hiro slipped my hand into his, and I turned around to face him, my heart pounding.

"Please trust me, Heaven. I don't want to fight with you. We have to work together to get through this."

"I know," I breathed, hardly daring to talk for fear of saying the wrong thing. "I do trust you. Absolutely."

"It's our fate. Our destiny."

Hiro raised his hand and touched my face, skirting my swollen eye and running his index finger down my cheekbone.

"Are you in pain?" he asked.

"No," I said, and thought, *Kiss me, kiss me, kiss me.*

Hiro cradled my chin delicately, and I closed my eyes, giving myself up to the warm touch of his hand on my face. I remembered all the times I had dreamed of just such a moment—now it was finally here.

"Good," Hiro said. He removed his hand from my face. My eyes flickered open. Hiro was looking out the window, his jaw tight. "We'd better have the driver stop a few streets away from your house—just to make sure we weren't followed from Vibe."

"Hiro," I whispered, disappointment seeping through me, "are you mad at me?"

Hiro turned around, and I saw that his face was tender. "No, Heaven, of course not," he said. "I just . . ." He turned away again.

"Yes?" I prompted, scootching a few centimeters closer to him on the seat.

"Maybe we could talk about this another time, okay?" Hiro cleared his throat, and his tone became more businesslike. "I'd really like to—just not now."

"Okay," I said, wanting desperately to press him but sensing that he needed his space. The disappointment couldn't ruin the deep core of warmth I still felt from Hiro's touch. Maybe he and Karen weren't such a sure thing after all.

The cab turned onto Dawson Street, and I stretched my legs in preparation for actually having to stand up. My muscles had turned from jelly to cement—it hurt just to straighten them out. I hoped that eventually I'd be able to come through a fight with a little more pep. That was one thing to focus on at least. I smiled to myself. I had to admit, being back with Hiro was great, but knowing that I'd be able to devote myself 100 percent to my training felt almost as good. I realized that I was nothing without my training. As Hiro had said, it was my path, and I couldn't deny that.

A few blocks from the house Hiro paid the driver and helped me out of the cab. He wrapped his arm around my waist, and I enjoyed the feeling of just having him close to me. As we walked in silence, I wondered if I should ask him in for a while. It would be comforting to have him around. I could make some tea, and we could all sit around in the living room and keep each other company. I even had a bag of rice crackers to snack on.

That was the first time I realized just how lonely the last couple of weeks had been.

"What's that?" Hiro asked, breaking the silence and pointing to a strange glow that rose in the distance. Almost simultaneously the sound of sirens filled the air. Two fire trucks rumbled by as Hiro and I sped up. A block later we could see police cars and more fire trucks clogging up the road and people coming out of their houses to watch the chaos unfold.

I instinctively grabbed Hiro's hand and we started to run. I forgot about my bashed-in face, my spent muscles. The sirens got louder as we sprinted down Dawson, the heat more intense.

As we got closer and closer, I let out a yell.

It was my house that was on fire. And Cheryl was trapped inside.

. . . A GIRL BORN
WITHOUT THE FEAR GENE

FEARLESS™

A SERIES BY
FRANCINE PASCAL

SIMON
PULSE

FROM SIMON PULSE
PUBLISHED BY SIMON & SCHUSTER

SIMON PULSE FICTION

Edgy, Daring, Real

Available now:

Coming soon:

"Well, we could grind our enemies into powder with a sledgehammer, but gosh, we did that last night."

—Xander

As long as there have been vampires, there has been the Slayer. One girl in all the world, to find them where they gather and to stop the spread of their evil...the swell of their numbers.

LOOK FOR A NEW TITLE EVERY MONTH!

Based on the hit TV series created by
Joss Whedon

2400

Aaron Corbet isn't a bad kid—he's just a little different.

On the eve of his eighteenth birthday, Aaron is dreaming of a darkly violent landscape. He can hear the sounds of weapons clanging, the screams of the stricken, and another sound that he cannot quite decipher. But as he gazes upward to the sky, he suddenly understands. It is the sound of great wings beating the air unmercifully as hundreds of armored warriors descend on the battlefield.

The flapping of angels' wings.

Orphaned since birth, Aaron is suddenly discovering newfound—and sometimes supernatural—talents. But not until he is approached by two men does he learn the truth about his destiny—and his own role as a liason between angels, mortals, and Powers both good and evil—some of whom are bent on his own destruction....

the
fallen

a new series by Thomas E. Sniegoski

Book One available March 2003

From Simon Pulse

Published by Simon & Schuster

AN AGELESS VENDETTA, AN ETERNAL LOVE, AND A DEADLY POWER . . .

"I'm living in a new town with a new family, and suddenly I'm discovering new powers, having new experiences, and meeting all sorts of new people. Including Jer. So why does it feel like I've known him forever? Even before I was born? It's almost like . . . magic."

WICKED

A new series about star-crossed lovers
from rival witch families

Book One: **WITCH**
Book Two: **CURSE**

Available From Simon Pulse